Marcenus R. K. Wright

The Only Hope

Marcenus R. K. Wright

The Only Hope

ISBN/EAN: 9783337090586

Printed in Europe, USA, Canada, Australia, Japan

Cover: Foto ©Andreas Hilbeck / pixelio.de

More available books at **www.hansebooks.com**

THE

ONLY HOPE:

OR,

TIME REVEALS ALL.

By MARCENUS R. K. WRIGHT,

AUTHOR OF "CONFUCIUS" AND THE "MASTERION."

CONTENTS:

" There are shades which will not vanish,
  There are thoughts thou canst not banish;
  Thou canst never be alone."
                              —*Byron.*

DETROIT, MICH.:
WM. GRAHAM, PRINTER, No. 52 BATES STREET.
1877.

OUR HOMESTEAD.

It consists of 30 acres of land, with good buildings, is located in the corporation of Middleville, Barry County, Michigan, and is

FOR SALE.

The land is in a fine state of cultivation, is well watered, has abundance of

YOUNG FRUIT TREES

growing upon it, as likewise an OLD BEARING ORCHARD, and is within one hundred rods of a railroad station.

Twenty acres of the land may be platted and sold for

BUILIDING LOTS,

at the option of the purchaser. Middleville now contains about 1,000 inhabitants, has a fine water-power, and is making a rapid and healthy growth.

The undersigned will arrange to sell

ONE HUNDRED SWARMS OF BEES

with the place, if desired. The bees will pay for it in three years, if properly cared for. All necessary instruction will be given for their management. Will give terms to suit purchaser.

Address, or see, as above,

MARCENUS WRIGHT.

THE

ONLY HOPE:

OR,

TIME REVEALS ALL.

By MARCENUS R. K. WRIGHT,

AUTHOR OF "CONFUCIUS" AND THE "MASTERION."

CONTENTS:

" There are shades which will not vanish,
There are thoughts thou canst not banish;
Thou canst never be alone.''
—*Byron.*

DETROIT, MICH.:
WM. GRAHAM, PRINTER, No. 52 BATES STREET.
1877.

Stereotyped by
Religio-Philosophical Publishing House,
Chicago, Ill.

PREFACE.

There are a great many curious things in the world to be considered. This little volume is one of them. The truth is, the author is a curious fellow himself. Should you doubt it, please peruse the pages of this pamphlet, and you will undoubtedly be convinced.

AUTOBIOGRAPHICAL.

A BRIEF NARRATIVE OF THE LIFE AND EXPERIENCE OF THE AUTHOR.

I am sorry to feel the necessity, dear reader, of taking my pen in my own hand to write concerning myself. The only excuse which I have to offer for so doing, is the fact that my experience during the past six or seven years, has been so remarkable, indeed, so absolutely beyond all that is ordinary, in the common course of life, that I reluctantly accept the task of making a written statement in regard to it.

I was born in the village of East Victor, Ontario County, in the State of New York, on the seventeenth day of December, 1830. From childhood I have been a confirmed mental *absentee* and *visionist*. This peculiarity of mind was, in my case, inherited ; my father and brother, as well as other members of our family being, "sleep-walkers," and, to use a Scriptural expression, "dreamers of dreams."

My brother, who long since departed this life, was more subject to these peculiar mental influences than the writer; but my father, who was an old-time Methodist preacher, and a great thinker, withal, was more given to the habit of "night-walking" than any member of his household.

It was not unusual for him to rise from his bed at night, in the state of somnambulism, and warm himself at the open fireplace in his old log cabin. At such times he would wander about the house, usually, without any apparent motive, yet, this was not always the case, for, upon many occasions, his mind seemed to definitely revert to subjects of daily thought. He would sometimes appear to be engaged in the occupation in which he employed his time. He would attempt to drive the cattle to water, or would strike at the oxen—as if driving them—which, during the day-time, he used in ploughing on his father's farm. He was, also, very fond of music, and would, now and then, try to give expression to his fond-ness for it, by attempting to sing some well-re-membered hymn. Occasionally he would open the door which led out into the yard in front of his dwelling. When this occurred, the cold air coming in contact with his person—in *dishabille* —usually aroused him from this irresponsible condition of trance, and he would return, cold and shivering, to his couch again.

When I was a small boy, as I think, only three years old, I distinctly remember of being subject to what are usually termed "waking-visions," or, in other words, I often observed objects and things which appeared real to my senses, yet, which other persons, who were near, did not seem to look at or notice. Sometimes these strange phantoms of the mind would make their *debut* in my presence very suddenly, and as often during the hours of the day as of those of the night.

' Now and then I would be looking out, perhaps, upon the road or street, being at home or in some familiar place, and would, all at once, observe some one near, whom I had met or known in years that were past, or, *so it seemed to me;* and yet these oft-recurring sights, these forms and faces would quickly vanish from my presence, leaving my mind in a state of great surprise and astonishment over the mystery or singularity of the event.

As I advanced in years, these fleeting apparitions were oftener observed, and became, as a general thing, more impressively objective in appearance. I was often very much astonished at their apparent substantiality, and I greatly wondered why it was that my mind was so peculiarly constituted as to be the lone recipient of such marked and unusual demonstrations.

During hours of sleep or repose, I realized many singular dreams, and enjoyed some of the most remarkable visions—visions which were often of the most imposing nature, embracing scenes which no language can describe—scenes in which the mind seemed to be carried away, as if in the full ecstacy and glory of a new and unspeakable revelation and life.

I was often in the habit of reflecting upon the subject of my own realizations. They were both extraordinary and uncommon. I thought, "How strange it is, that in this peculiar mental state, the intelligent part of my being is able to grasp great thoughts, give expression to quaint and rare ideas, realize all the emotions of joy, sorrow, pity, contempt and anger, or reason, and observe with such minute accuracy and skill," and I was puzzled and perplexed.

I began to look upon my experience in a most singular light. I could but regard myself as either very much favored or greatly bedeviled in mind. My spirit seemed to be incessantly traveling about nights in this entranced condition. I was visiting with friends or meeting with strangers. I was continually engaged in some sport or duty; would be playing or quarreling with my boyish companions; would, unluckily, fall into some bees' nest, or, what is still worse, be compelled to seek refuge from enormous serpents and ferocious wild beasts, which I frequently encountered in these "midnight rambles of the spirit."

After years of thoughtful consideration upon the subject of these unusual occurrences, I become convinced—of what seemed to me to be very likely to be true—that I was either an object of unusual solicitude, somehow, in some mysterious way, or, that in an individual capacity, I was either graciously or morbidly endowed with a self-acting genius of intelligence.

I began to think, at last, in view of the fact, that, upon several occasions, I had what the good folks at home called the "nightmare," when I was really quite well—that the elements and forces of my mind were prompted to action, or were acted upon, by some unseen, yet conscious thought-directing power.

I was much inclined to accept the idea or doctrine—one which was sometimes advanced by my friends as a possible explanation of much of the phenomena to which I was subject—of the presence and protecting care of "guardian watchers" or beings of another and a higher life. I was quite satisfied, in my own judgment, that the influences which I realized—as *emotional* or *impulsive*—were emphatically distinct from any feeling or feelings which arose from the natural operation of my own senses. Indeed, they seemed, in every instance, to act as an intimating or propelling force, somewhat difficult to resist ; and, moreover, I discovered that in yielding to them, without objection, I usually met with satisfactory success in my daily labors and undertakings.

But here, with the reader's permission, I will revert to a circumstance which I am inclined to think has had much to do with my many singular, pleasant and unpleasant lessons in somnambulism and *abseneistic** visions.

When I was a boy, being only seven years old, I met with a somewhat serious accident. My brother, who was of a very restless and enthusiastic temperament, and who was some five years older than myself, was engaged with other lads of his own age, in ball-playing in the garden near my father's house. Through youthful curiosity, and a desire to catch the ball, I inadvertantly drew too near my brother, who, at the time, held the bat—which was made of solid wood—in his hands. As the ball was thrown for him to strike at, he swung the club backward over his left-side

---

* This term is used in preference to the word clairvoyance. It is not a positive phrase, and signifies "apart," or a "retiring from."

with terrible force, and I, being in the way, unavoidably received the blow, which fell exactly
over my eyes and the region of my perceptive
faculties.

I was felled to the ground blind and sense-
less. My father came and carried me into the
house. My mother was frightened, but with my
sisters labored assiduously to restore my mind to
consciousness and relieve me from pain. My
brother wept as he saw me lying insensible upon
a bed of suffering. Several days elapsed before
I fully recovered my sight. My mind was im-
paired. I realized an indefinite action of my
thoughts. My senses appeared, at times, to be
greatly obtused or fluctuating. It seemed as
though I could not hold the organic action of my
mind under the control of my will. This was a
most singular phenomenon, but it gradually dis-
appeared. Years passed on, and, as I grew to
manhood, I naturally thought less of what had
happened. I was young, and the vivaciousness
of my youth tended to prevent my attaching any
very serious consequence to my misfortune; yet,
such was the effect of the injury which I had sustained, that I could perceive a marked change in
the capacity of my memory.

Six years subsequent to the occurrence of this
event, my brother, who had been a great sufferer
from lameness and disease for a period embracing nearly three years, died, leaving me, the
youngest child of my father's family, to mourn
his untimely loss, and, in after years, to bear the
burden of many household cares.

My attachment to my brother, notwithstanding

his decease, seemed not in the least degree cut off or forgotten; but, on the contrary, a constant yearning and aspiration to reach a knowledge of his condition or state of being, inspired my thoughts, and carried my reflections away in fancy, to some heavenly realm, as I inferred, wholly beyond my ability to comprehend.

For many years subsequent to my brother's death, it seemed to me as though I could sense his presence, or realize his nearness, at times, through certain strange feelings and influences which descended upon me like a charm, as if to guide my efforts, or put me on my guard against personal mistakes and misfortunes. Indeed, I was the recipient of many evidences, both by day and by night, which tended to confirm my mind in my already well-established belief, in the presence and watchful care of "angel missionaries."

In the Summer of 1848, I was invited, by a friend, to go and investigate—as I could avail myself of leisure time—the then new and somewhat marvelous "spiritual manifestation." Notwithstanding I was laughed at by some of my acquaintances and my family at home for my determination to do so, I did not let the opportunity pass, but went to work in real earnest to that end.

In company with the Rev. Charles Hammond, of Rochester, N. Y., I visited the celebrated Fox Family, who were then residing in that city, and listened to the "mysterious sounds" which occurred in their presence. Subsequently my father's house was made the scene of some of the most remarkable demonstrations. A medium for the physical phases of the phenomena—than whom I have never known one better—visited our home and remained in our family during a period of several months.   Upon this occasion it was my good fortune to gain access to a knowledge of these peculiar manifestations, which encompassed nearly the whole subject, in its external aspect, and settled the question as to their origin, in my mind, forever.

In the Autumn of 1867 my father died, having attained the ripe old age of eighty-four years. My mother, one sister and myself, now constituted all that were left of our family, which had formerly consisted of eight members.

As a consequence of my father's death, I became, at times, quite sad and lonely. The many cares which it fell to my lot to bear were weighty and troublesome to my mind. I felt that I was, virtually, "alone in the world," struggling onward in the pathway of personal duty, compelled to think for myself, and to repose confidence in my own judgment and efforts.

It is true, that I was not without some means to comfort me in life; but the absence of five members of our once united and joyous household, caused me to realize a depression of heart and spirit, which I found it extremely painful to endure.

I became each day more serious and thoughtful. I felt as if there was a strange vacancy around me. The creeping vine, which grew beside the window, over the lattice, was less attractive and inviting. The beautiful flowers, lining the walk which led from our dwelling to the open street, failed to impart that joy and happiness which they had been wont to confer. The circle of loved ones who met to enjoy the evening's repast, was no longer as blithesome and cheerful as in days that were gone. I was reminded of the fact, that life presented many anomalous phases and features. Instead of being a restless and rollicksome boy, as I had been, I was obliged to think with greater earnestness and deliberation, and also to look after many important interests.

In the year 1868, or immediately after the death of my father, I left my native village, in the State of New York, and journeying to the West, settled in Middleville, Barry County, Michigan, where my family still reside.

It was in this place, and sometime after we located there, that through a circumstance, I was thrown into the abnormal or entranced state of mind, a condition from which I did not fully recover within a year and eight months.*

During that period, which really seemed to me like an age, I passed through an experience, in superinduced mental action, which no language is fully adequate to explain. I was tossed and tumbled, in thought, like the billows of the ocean. My realizations were generally more distressing than pleasant. My mind was actually *caught* and *imprisoned*, so to say, psychologically, by a wary *Aniwone*, or guardian spirit, whose intention it was to answer as far as practicable, to my solicitation for communion with friends in the immortal world.

---

* See a work by the author, entitled "The Mastereon."

My mental faculties were played upon during my waking hours without cessation, even as a pianist would play upon his favorite instrument. So fully did the unseen influence possess control of my nervous sensibilities and the action of my mind, that for weeks and months together, it seemed to me as if my body and brain were *actualized* in the very life and intellect of some transcendent mind or "Deity of the Air."

Every feeling and desire, every emotion natural to my being, every sense and ability which I possessed, was pushed into activity, or masked and unmasked in a series of realizations, at once truly marvelous and impressive.

My mind was in a condition, which is known to mesmerists, as a state in which there is an almost perfect "psychologic subjectability of the senses." I retained but partial control of my own mental functions and powers. I was constrained to utter words, sentences, prose and poetry, in strange language and in syllabic forms, which I could not comprehend, and that for weeks and months in succession. I was pretty much the subject of another's will—the invisible *Aniwone* of the "life immortal."

During the lengthened period of fifteen months, with the exception of short intervals, a most powerful as well as unpleasant pressure rested upon the *top of my head*. A strong current of mental elements, proceeding from my celestial magnetizer, descended upon and entered the various labyrinths of my brain, grasping, as if by an *astringent* force, its very atoms, and causing my thoughts to act in a manner conformable to, yet quite different from their ordinary movements, as appointed under the directing influence of my own will.

Gradually I began to hear a "still, small voice" whispering words and sentences *in my mind.* This speech or conversation, although given without vocal sounds, was the same in articulation, in every modulation of expression—as addressed to the consciousness of hearing affixed in the soul— as that given by oral communication.

This was a most wonderful phenomenon, and for a time I doubted the reality of my own experience. The idea that I could hear an *invisible* person or being addressing me, and that distinctly, and at the same time be engaged listening to the conversations of those near me in this life, was not only a source of anxiety and serious reflection, but as well of sad and unsettled convictions. I soon become satisfied that, for some reason which I could not fully fathom, I had become the possessor of a most marvelous gift—*that of a twofold or double hearing.* The one was sonorous and common, the other was inaudible and of rare occurrence. Both were the same in their effect upon the ear, and both conveyed the same impression to the understanding, as a result of thought and utterance.

I felt somewhat embarrassed in consequence of the newness of my situation. The impartations of the spirit soon become tedious and irksome. I began to think that, like Socrates, I was accompanied by a "familiar demon," or that, like the Nazarene, during his prolonged temptation, I had fallen into questionable company, and was being betrayed by his atrocious majesty himself. It was not until many weeks had passed, and I had endured much pain and anguish of heart, that my *inner hearing* become fully and perfectly established. I was a great sufferer from the over-action of my mental forces. My thoughts were but measurably under my own control. I became much emaciated as a result of the influence which was held over my appetites and intellectual powers. The incipient conversations and speech to which I was obliged to listen, was often a great source of annoyance. It was, truly, the greatest punishment that I ever realized in all my life.

I lost forty-one pounds of flesh while I was passing through this strange transition in psychology. The pressure upon the top of my head became so great at times, that I adopted the plan of wearing a *heavy mask* for self-protection. I was also very angry at intervals, in spite of myself, and abused the *agents* who so persistently domineered over the action of my senses. I here frankly acknowledge that I harrowed up the "Kings' English," and forgot every "Christian precept" while in this peculiar mental mood.

The "invisibles" bestowed upon me the customary chastisement for an approach to the *real*, as regards a knowledge of the "future life."* While being benefited in mind I was likewise being cajoled by words of promise and flattery. I knew my own situation very well, but was unable to gain relief. In a serious passion of purpose I concluded to rid myself of the whole spiritual

---

* History furnishes no instance where a person, receiving gifts of this nature, has not had to endure similar trials.

business, and return once more, if possible, to my normal and natural state of mind.

I was sad and subdued, but as willful as Cæsar. In my distress and anxiety I took up my pen and appealed to Andrew Jackson Davis, the distinguished author and seer, by letter, for advice and counsel. Mr. Davis maintained a very ominous silence. One day, several weeks after I had written him, however, I received a very pleasant letter from his wife. It was a source of comfort to my care-worn and hopeless spirit, but it afforded me no relief from the mental trials which so distressed and annoyed me. At the time to which I allude, I would willingly have sacrificed all I possessed in the world to have secured my freedom from spirit control.

My condition was truly lamentable. My thoughts were propelled into rapid and incessant action, day after day and week after week, without regard to my feelings or desires. This was the state of mind which I realized most of the time, while awake; when I slept I became entranced, and my senses were exalted or carried into visions, the most ecstatic and grand.

Four months subsequent to the time when I wrote to Mr. Davis, I was, in good part, relieved from the unpleasantness which pertained to my psychological realizations. I had gazed into the heavens with spirit-awakened sight, or as permitted under the restraints enforced by the *Kamowanse*.* The laws of mind, the origin and destiny of man, the Spirit-world, its place and

---

* Supervisors of the guardian realm.

position, as likewise, the future of the departed, were questions which had been met and answered to my entire satisfaction.

Thus the brother, whom I had loved in my youth, had returned and spoken with me from his immortal home. He had taught me, by a severe lesson, not only that his life had been made secure in a higher sphere of existence, but, that to commune with me in the full freedom of speech, was an act reprehensible in the presence of the *Ghoamoni** of the Air.

I was now contented but not happy. I had been permitted to gaze through the darksome folds of outer nature into the realm beyond ; and while I had learned many things which tended to exalt my feelings and improve my understanding, I had, likewise, discovered very serious cause for trouble and suffering in "the life to come." Matters were not all pleasant and agreeable "over the border," as I had hoped that they might be. The Spirit-land, I found, was a home of misery as well as of blessedness. I saw that the Christian's idea of "retribution" hereafter, was in a measure true ; that the soul, as a conscious entity, was constantly reprehended, both through observation and knowledge gained.

Among the *Tolena*,† on the heights of *Comlan*,‡ not far from my earthly home, my brother lived. His life, I perceived, had been greatly changed. His appearance was not as it had been.

---

* A wise fraternity in Spirit-life, who manifest opposition to "familiar" or unremedial intercourse with mortals.

† Those who bend downward in sympathy.

‡ An aerial stratification where numerous spirits dwell.

His soul-body was unlike the former physical structure. I recognized his nearness through imparted sympathy. Although unseen, I could detect his presence by a kindred similarity of sense, of speech, of intonation and utterance; even as we sometimes know a friend by his walk, or some peculiar habit, so, at times, I could realize my brother's approach and know of his attentions.*

But what was the cause of his return to the mundane world? What had induced him to reveal to me so much of the nature of his life, as a spirit in the "immortal sphere beyond?" I was both grief-stricken and surprised. My mind was overwhelmed with joy and astonishment. I wondered why others were not permitted to hold communion with the departed, in a manner similar to myself. I thought of the Christian Apostles attended by their "angel visitants." I thought of Socrates with his "demon guide." I remembered Swedenborg with his accompanying "spiritguard" and "wonderful visions."

Was I to be the recipient of angel favors? Was I to suffer for having received a knowledge of my immortal destiny? I had already experienced a serious inconvenience for having attempted to reach that object. How long was I to be teased and tried? How long was I to be led on in uncertainty of my fate?

---

* It is customary with the dead to represent themselves, commonly—both in dreams and visions—as they appeared in the physical form upon earth. This is done so that we may recognize them. The question, "What is the real form of the spirit," is one of serious moment, and one which the writer has referred to, briefly, in the essay in this pamphlet entitled the "Immersed Life."

I remembered the Scriptures, and how Jesus of Nazareth was led up into a high mountain to be "tempted" by the "Evil One." I thought of Jacob, and how he wrestled with the angel at Penial. My mind reverted to Swedenborg's first vision, in which he was taunted by the Devil—who appeared in one corner of the room in which he was dining—for eating too much supper. I remembered the phantasmagorical figures seen by the half-entranced M. Nicoli. I thought of A. J. Davis, and of his traveling upwards of eighty miles—over the hills and through the valleys west of the Hudson river, near Poughkeepsie, N. Y. —in a very brief period of time, while in a trance. I was reminded of the words of Job: "Then thou scarest me with dreams, and terrifiest me through visions," and I wondered at what had passed.

Were my trials and vexations to be like unto theirs? Were the lessons imparted to my mind, from spirit sources, to become a cause of smothered misery? I began to see that it cost *pains* and *penalties*, to *deal with the dead*.

I reflected upon the subject of my position and circumstances in life. I thought of my happy home and its pleasant surroundings, of my wife and children, and friends, and I wept with fear and grief.

My family were anxious for my welfare. I had imparted to them, as far as I was able, a knowledge of my situation, and the discoveries which I had made. They were desirous to have me relinquish all relationship with the spiritual opportunities of my life. I was willing to gratify them as well as to arrive at some settled state of mind.

But how was it to be accomplished? I was a subject of psychology, of somnambulism, of trance, of natural clairvoyance, of spirit-hearing. What could I do? The instrument is not the chooser of the music to which it gives expression. I could not consistently forbid a power which had quietly led me on in life with a guardian purpose, which, from my childhood, had guided my footsteps, in kindness, and with success, to me, in my dealings with the world.

My researches had proved to my entire satisfaction, that the human soul was immortal, or continued to exist, with conscious knowledge of its own identity after death. I was fully persuaded, in my own mind, that my brother lived. His return to, and communion with me, was as unexpected as it was marvelous or unusual in the common course of individual experience. There was something mysterious in his very presence, and especially in his condescension; which, although not always familiar, was kindly accessible.

But what was his object? Did he simply wish to let me know that he lived? Had he any blessing to confer? Had he any secret to reveal? Aye; it was his knowledge, gained by observation, by watching the movements of my mental forces, during many years, that the blow which he had inflicted upon me, by accident, with the ball-club, in my youth, had left a lasting and injurious impression upon my memory, or its *foci* of concentration.

One day as I sat musing upon what had passed, he very pleasantly spoke to me and said :—

"My brother, we are living in quiet and peaceful enjoyment in the *Remeoni* of the 'superior realm.' Your sisters, Caroline, Jennett and Julia, together with myself, have remained in our respective aerial *Jottans*, during most of the time since our departure from the terrestrial world. Sometimes we have wandered, for a season, over the heights of the atmosphere, to view the various races and nations of the earth, but usually the home of our past worldly cares, friendships, attachments and devotion, is the sacred *Syzygian* place, to which we are confidently bound, in the performance of guardian duties.

"I come back to you, my brother, through obedience to a feeling or principle of mind, quite well understood, but seldom made practical in human life. The unfortunate blow which you received at my hands, when a boy, and which temporarily deprived you of your consciousness, gave me much cause for distress and uneasiness when I became a spirit.

"Some four years after my entrance into the bright realm of immortality, a friend and associate, in whom I placed both trust and confidence, pointed out to me in the movements of your mind, a *deflection* in the power of memory, which I discovered was caused by that unhappy circumstance. My soul bowed down in sorrow when I realized what I had done, and I resolved that I would serve you with greater freedom, *for the sad fate which resulted from a blow.*

"It was not this alone, however, which induced me to speak with you. There are, still, other reasons which time may reveal. Be peaceful, quiet, kind, generous and just, and you will realize greater happiness from our presence, and be more contented and better blessed in mind.

"When we think it advisable we will grant you a commission to aid in disseminating a better knowledge of our state of existence. We will produce phenomena in your presence, and supply other suggestive means to prove that we not only live, but that we often approach and render valuable assistance to our trusting friends upon earth.

"The spirit, my brother, is a law unto itself. In our life the *Homonse*, or ministers *defacto* in our *medewansa*, being worthy counselors, in all that concerns our relationship to mankind, justly hamper, by *rules of mystery*, that familiarity in intercourse with us, which the unthoughtful and the unwise among men would seem to solicit.

"No case of absolutely free and unrestrained intercourse as between the two worlds, was ever yet permitted. The guard of *Konovorson*, a dutiful spirit soldiery—in a mental sense—preside over all the interests which relate to our communion with mankind, and we all quietly and willingly obey the decisions which they demand to have enforced. At the present time there is somewhat of a relaxation, however, in regard to these matters, and more freedom is allowed to the 'guardian hosts of the air.'

"As concerns our wisdom, it is, truly, unknown to man. We are ever happy to speak a kindly word with those who approach us in an earnest and worthy manner; still, our intercourse with the nether sphere, is, as it must ever continue to be, governed by our situation and the knowledge which we possess of individual needs and characteristics.

"The felicitous privilege of existence which we inherit, being — to mankind — inappreciable, is generally looked upon as an insecure expectation. Many, as we observe, even doubt the possibility of an 'immortal life.' Sorrowfully, though I say it, money is made 'the king in all council,' and the obligations which repose in its use, to surely combine to suppress the truth as well as to stultify the operations of justice.

"The turbid power of wealth, and the distinctions which its possession confers, are a sad comment upon human intelligence and practical righteousness. The angels of the *Parinola** must long continue to weep over the arrogance and folly of men, if money is not confined to the more legitimate uses to which it may be applied. We hope, that in a few years, the people of the earth will be willing to listen to our 'better counsels,' and be guided to a haven of safety, in all their dealings with each other. The work of reformation is likely to try the strongest hearts, but we confidently believe that reason will triumph, and that wisdom will eventually preside over all the interests which pertain to the lot of mortals.

"Be patient, my brother, trusting in righteousness as a dominant law. Through friendship, with us, you have learned that there is *no death*. You have listened to the 'still, small voice' of the 'ministering watcher' above. When you

---

* The dwelling place of many long-time residents over the earth. Home of exalted equality.

ask, we answer. Be at peace with yourself and the world, and fear not."

In concluding this narrative of my personal experience—a statement which is necessarily very brief—I will but add that as I was born a somnambule, so, by the aid of another, I have attained to that condition of mind which is known or designated as "natural clairvoyance." At times I am the recipient of the most delightful as well as the most suggestive visions. I also hear the dead speak to me, whenever, by request or desire, I solicit their conversations. So far as visions are concerned I little regard them as responsible in what they often represent. While they are, many times, grand, beautiful and instructive, they are, no doubt, purely a result of the transmission and imprinting of thought—through will-force or psychologic processes—upon the mind of the sensitive subject of trance. This is done by the spirit guardian, who is ever near. Dreams are of the same nature. These are imparted to the mind in the same manner, but are, usually, a good deal manipulated by the invisible operator, to conceal his own presence, which is the wisdom of the spirit. As regards *Clairaudiance* or "spirit hearing,"* it is more gratifying and responsible—affording means for pleasant and agreeable communion with our departed friends, and yet, this gift is not without its pains and penalties, and, in certainty, can not become very common among men.

---

* The author has not yet placed himself in a position to use his "spirit-hearing" for the gratification of others, save in a few instances. It is now his pleasure to think, however, that, ere long, he may be so situated that he can.

It is now nearly six years since I first listened to the speech of spirits. Sometimes they impart their ideas and thoughts without the use of words, at others by the use of language, as we do in common conversation among ourselves. There is a wide difference between these two methods of communication. The first is pure, representing exactly what the mind wishes to convey; the second is subject, of course, to all the variable and deceptive meanings which the use of words engenders or enables the mind to employ.

My personal realizations have been the cause of considerable self-suffering. I find that it is not "all gold that glitters." To be a Spiritualist is a very easy matter, but to possess the gifts of a seer is a dear-bought privilege, whatever may be the opinions of the uninitiated in regard to the matter.

So far as I am individually concerned, if what I have herein stated is true, the reader will readily concede that, in all probability, I have made some little progress in regard to discoveries which relate to a "future life."

This is, indeed, true; and yet I am reluctant to communicate much that I have learned, or to openly reveal the nature of the knowledge which I have gained.

Suffice it to say, that, although I am compelled to differ with some of the best thinkers, seers and philosophers of the past, as well as of the present time, and that, in regard to several very important questions, I am, nevertheless, quite unwilling to engage in any wrangle of words over spiritual matters, and have not the slightest wish to change the religious opinions of others, save in so far as truth and evidence may substantiate the wisdom of such a purpose.

I give the facts, as herein presented, for the benefit of those who desire to investigate mental or metaphysical phenomena, and I sincerely trust that, in so doing, I shall have rendered some service to the world.

THE IMMERSED LIFE.

A PHILOSOPHICAL DISSERTATION UPON THE STATE
OF THE DEAD.

The subject of the condition of the immortal spirit, its manner of life and power of locomotion, are themes of thought, which, although somewhat difficult of pursuit, are, nevertheless, really deserving of our most serious and earnest attention.

While it is true that the consideration of any and all metaphysical problems, inevitably leads the mind into realms of irksome and discouraging research, yet, inasmuch as the laws of nature are everywhere a unit in their application to and control of living objects, and as a principle of analogy is inseparably associated with the movements of matter, in all of its diversified forms, we may no doubt arrive at many just and legitimate conclusions concerning them, even without the benefit of sight, by processes of reasoning alone.

It is hardly possible to conceive of, or realize, what the human soul or spirit is, yet certain we are that it is organically formed, that it is a counterpart of the material body, and a unification of the life-elements of nature.

Knowledge, thought, reflection, personal consciousness and activity could not exist without some kind of organic form through which to find expression.

This is not only the case with the spirit in its connection with the external world, but the same conditions are equally required, and the same argument will equally apply to the death-delivered mind or individual.

The atmosphere of the earth is a transparent medium. We can not see its substance, although we realize its presence. It is a vast body of limpid ethers, yet it is wholly beyond the reach of our vision.

The human soul or spirit is also beyond the reach of outward observation, but that it has a method of existence and a form peculiar to itself, is as well to be inferred, and as unquestionably true, as though the whole matter were apparent to the sense of sight.

As the ocean, with its tumbling waters, contains innumerable organic forms, which are conditioned to life in its ever-changing elements, so, invisible to our perception, may the all-encompassing aerial realm, beyond the clouds, be peopled by communities of unseen spirit-beings, or by nations corresponding to those of the earth.

But upon the hypotheses of the presence of immortal dwellers in the surrounding atmosphere of our planet, we are unavoidably led to the conclusion, that the form of the spirit must be essentially changed, so far as its resemblance to the mortal body is concerned, in order to meet the demands of a purely *immersed* state of life.

Andrew Jackson Davis has stated, in one of his volumes, "That a stratum of atmosphere, more or less dense, is always necessary for the spiritual organism to stand or walk upon," thereby implying that spirits are not only possessed of legs and feet, but that their means of locomotion is dependent upon their use.

Now let us examine this proposition, and see whether it agrees with reason, or is likely to become established as true, in the light of probable cause and effect. Let us see how it will appear as compared with an earthly condition of existence, which is fixed and local, and one which is purely transient and unstable, as that of living in an ever restless or moving medium.

Upon the earth we can stand still or move at our pleasure. We can lie down to rest and when we wake we find ourselves in the same place. Now, how is it with the spirit? It is in the air. It is not *open* but *within* a sea of ethers, which are in constant motion.

There is nothing in space to take hold of or lay down by. There is not a material object visible in the whole realm of the aerial sea above us. Even the clouds find no place for delay.

What is there in the air for a spirit to stand upon? Aye; but you say, the air itself. Nay! it were impossible! It would move from beneath your feet, and, moreover, the spirit is, or must be, itself, kept constantly in motion by the wafting power of its ever unsettled elements.

A stratum of air, we are told, is necessary for

the spirit to stand or walk upon. Is there any safety in a proposition so vague and indefinite?

The atmosphere is wholly of a conformable nature, as well as *transitory and interblending* in every part. It has no surfacial layers in any local sense.

There are no doubt aerial currents as there are ocean streams, and it is well known, that in elevated regions, the air is more pure and refined than in positions near the surface of the earth.

But this does not change the nature of the case. Refined matter in motion and granulated substance in a state of inertia or repose, are two very different things. We know that we can walk and that we can stand, because we rest upon a solid basis; but to suppose that a spirit is subject to corresponding conditions, would be to put the finishing stroke of folly upon all arguments of inference or analogy, and, moreover, such an hypothesis is as needless, as in the light of nature's rigid laws, it is absurd and insecure.

Every living thing in creation is adapted to its peculiar form and state of existence, and the Divine builder has, in every case, appointed means exactly suited to meet the purpose and privilege of being, and this principle will, no doubt, apply quite as well to the living spirit in immortal realms as to the visible creatures of the external world.

When, in the event of death, the soul is released from its material covering, and rises up into the atmosphere to dwell, if ever such an event takes place, it is self-evident, that the change thus experienced, is brought about through conformity to established law, and that every result or attendant circumstance is, or should be, perfectly consistent therewith. To live within the open sea of flowing ethers, which surround the terrestrial world, or even in the space beyond, would require a most marvelous revolution, not only in the ordinations and appointments of life, but in the form of the spirit as compared to the physical body.

There are two principles, represented in the out-workings of the system of nature, which must be complied with, by all creatures that live either a temporary or permanent life within moving spheres—as water and air. One of these is the existence of a law of equilibrium, as between the physical body and the water or atmosphere wherein they exist; the other, is the adaptation of the dependent form to the various grades of specific gravity, which belong to the different liquids and fluids, which are the mediums of contaminate life.

For example, consider the variability of the tribes of the sea. They are possessed of marked and marvelous distinctions; and although residing in an element essentially uniform in its general qualities, still they are separated into numerous divisions, and confined to special localities. Some live in small streams, others in large rivers; some in marshes, others in bays and lakes; some in fresh water, while others are restricted to that of a more dense and briny quality. The waters of Oneida Lake, for example, are peculiarly adapted to the development and life of the Catfish, the Eel and the Bull-head, while the pure springs, streams

and lakes, of more northern New York, are peopled, almost exclusively, by the Salmon and the
Speckled Trout.

Then, again, we see that, as the fishes live in a
restless medium, they are peculiarly adapted to
that form of existence which they have received
at the hand of nature. The suspension of fish in
water, their ability to float in it without sinking
to the bottom, like a piece of lead or other heavy
substance, is owing to the fact that their bodies
are so formed as to rest in equilibrium of weight
anywhere within its confines.

The fish species are uniformly buoyed up by
the water, for the reason that they have been
created in a manner well adapted to life in that
liquid. But to meet every difficulty in the case,
such as the variability of gravity or that which
arises from water in turbulent motion, these animals have been provided with an instrument or
bladder, which receives or emits atmospheric air,
according to circumstances and their situation.

What a wonderful provision! What a remarkable gift from the hand of the Divine maker, is
this mechanical *artificeum*, in the middle of the
fishes' body, which can be so easily contracted
or expanded at pleasure. "The fishes," says the
learned Borelli, "are better and easier sustained
by the water, in which they live, than we are by
the earth upon which we tread. They have not
the fatigue of supporting their own weight as we
have, need no feet, like quadrupeds and fowls,
and experience no lassitude from standing."

Thus we see how nicely adapted all water-abid-
ing animals are to the medium of life in which

they exist. The water is their home, and in it they find comfort and happiness. But suppose we take a fish from the limpid stream in which it is so comfortable, and clipping its ventral fins close to its body, return it again to its native element. What do we discover? Only this! a fish having no power to support an upright position. By the brandishing of its tail it is thrown forward, but it turns and it twists, and its rectilinear course and uprightness can no longer be maintained. In this we are reminded of the grandeur of that system of nature which so perfectly provides means to meet all existing demands.

But what of the released spirit? What of the immortal soul that has parted from its terrestrial moorings? The atmosphere is its inevitable home, at all events, for many years, and, perhaps, for centuries. The qualities of atmospheric air are peculiarly combinaceous and translucent. It is 780 times lighter than water, and the constituent ingredients of which it is composed, vary, as we rise from the surface of the earth.

Air is a purely invisible medium, possessing both the qualities of weight and compressibility. Its tendency to a downward pressure, and the effect of that pressure upon any given object, is altogether determined by the character of the object itself, and, then again, we find that this principle of pressure decreases as we ascend mountainous elevations or rise in a balloon.

The smoke which ascends from the household chimney, or which rises from the burning forest, mounts the atmosphere to a certain altitude, which may be called its balancing position, and there it rests or floats at ease.

From this it will appear, that invisible beings, who may inhabit the aerial regions above us in countless numbers, although unseen and inscrutable to our comprehension, must necessarily conform to fixed laws of life—to conditions which pertain to matter in its more refined and imponderable forms.

The question of the situation of the Spirit-world, the manner in which spirits live, and the organic form with which they are possessed or endowed, are all interesting subjects for our contemplation.

To the consistent thinker there is no longer any doubt as to the materiality of the elements of mind. The activity of the faculties of thought, the stern edicts of the principle of will, in its control of the physical form and contention with outward nature, furnish satisfactory evidence of its substantial characteristics.

To suppose, as many do, that the spirit or mind is in every sense immaterial, is to conclude that its existence is lost in its own refinement, or rendered inconceivable as a result of the attenuation of its own substance. But this is not true. The spirit is a being of parts, and, like every creature in the temple of the universe, must hold to its own form of being ; and, although it has passed beyond the reach of outward perception, it is the more wonderful as the recipient of a fluidescent destiny in more exalted realms.

When we are informed, as we often are, by many sincere and well meaning thinkers, that, upon our departure from the external world, we are at liberty to traverse indiscriminately the boundless dominions of the Infinite universe, we have only to look to the fundamental principles governing matter in its diversified forms, and its established methods of association, to realize the utter fallaciousness of such a statement.

All things existing upon the surface of the earth are fashioned from the material ingredients of which it is composed. The centralization of the spiritized elements of the mind, is a result brought about by organic growth, and these elements are quite as dependent upon nature, for support and continuance in life, as the grosser substance of the corporeal body itself.

We may imagine that the departed soul is free, chaste, and unrestrained in its privilege of being; that it is superior to the influences which hold a universe in subjection, or which control matter in its more exalted states of refinement; but such an inference is demonstrably false, in view of the fact, that there is no place for relief from the forces and powers of creation anywhere within the boundless ocean of immensity.

The spirit, we say, is organically formed. It rises from the earth to dwell in a region of aerial joys and pleasures, but it can not travel beyond that position which the "line of life" determines.* There is a "stay law," regulating and limiting, to strict boundaries, every particle of substance of which our planet is composed. The stratifications of the earth, as likewise the concen-

---

* See sketch, by Prof. Louis Agassiz, on the subject of "The Natural Provinces of the Animal World," in a work entitled, "Types of Mankind."

tric belts of the surrounding atmosphere, are rigidly held to their place and position by binding laws, or by their inherent gravitational force.

All living creatures, as we have before intimated, receive the blessing of existence within a confined radius or sphere, beyond which they can not reach, above which they can not rise. When the spirit is freed from its casket of clay, and goes out to enjoy the successes which attend its mission in a new and improved form of existence, we may say that it has triumphed, that it has won a great and substantial victory, that it has, in the fullest degree, mastered the imperfections which belong to outward life ; but we may not say that it is absolutely free, or, that it is not confined to regions and positions determined by its condition as a being of dependent life.

The action of light and heat, the force of gravity, or the laws of attraction and repulsion, are omnipotent influences, and control every particle of matter in existence. The alluvial soils cling to the surface of the earth, the waters repose upon its bosom, while the mists and clouds rise and float along the arch of the sky, within the limit determined by their density and composition.

All refined elements, all spiritized ingredients, must inevitably obey the commands of mother nature. When the solid substance of gold, silver, iron, or any other metal, is rendered so hot, by fire or electrical transmission, as to become wholly volatilized, passing away and disappearing from our sight in the surrounding air —as boiling water evaporates and floats away unseen—it only finds a new place in creation, a new

position in the vast arcana of material relationships, to which it is assigned by associative and
governing principles of power latent in all atoms.

The human spirit is an organization of the
*Reneze*** of matter, and as such, can be but little
more refined than the ethers and substances from
which it derives its support and maintenance in
being. The electric element which flouts and
plays in the sky with maddening force, which
leaps from cloud to cloud with fierce motion,
which decends to the earth with strength to prostrate the giant forms of the forest, is, perhaps,
quite as refined as mental principles, or the active
energy of the nervous system. Certain we are,
that it is equally invisible to our perception, as
an associative and permeating force, and, as
well, in nature equally remote from our comprehension.

What a happy idea it is to think, that when we
leave the material body behind us, in the event of
death, we shall become beings of ethereal life;
that the form which we shall then wear, will be so
light, so buoyant, that we may rise to the most
refined stratifications of the encompassing atmosphere, there to rest in ease, comfort and happiness—floating, like the fish of the sea, in the restless rivers of the air, to gain a knowledge of the
wisdom of God.

But, perhaps we may think that we can escape
the decrees of omnipotence, that we can override
the laws of creation, and stand above every influence which holds a universe in restraint. Perhaps we may think that the spirit is *nothing*, is

---

* Renewing life.

not substance, is simply an unsubstantial vapor, an ideal principle, which amounts to a defeat in whatever it *is*, or *is not*.

To those who entertain *such* thoughts, or, who harbor such sentiments, there is a prospect for a strange disappointment in the future, for such are surely at fault in their discernment, and will, one day, reap the reward of their short-sightedness.

The blue heavens above us are not an open void. The sky is not a vacuum in which only emptiness is to be found. Nature contains no waste places, no vacancies.

The soil we tread upon is substance ! The water we drink is substance ! The air we breathe is substance ! The vital life of the spirit is derived from the innate and essential essence of matter, and "the principle of will," which controls the organic intellect of the human mind, presents the self-evident demonstration of its accommodating materiality.

It is neither a good reason to assert that a thing or a being does not exist because we do not see it, nor that it can not, and be invisible ; and it is a still greater evidence of folly to suppose that because a thing, substance or being is unseen, it is conse-quently *immaterial*, and has no place or purpose in the designs of creation.

Spiritualism has clearly demonstrated the fact, that every human soul is immortal, and reason, following up the vast accumulation of evidence in its support, has established the concurrent fact, that the home of the immortal spirit is not, as it can not be, very distant from the earth.

If spirits lived beyond the atmosphere of our

world—just think of it—they would, in order to become "ministering watchers," be obliged to travel at the rapid rate of nineteen miles per second ; one thousand one hundred and forty miles per hour ; thirteen thousand six hundred and eighty every day ; four hundred and sixty-four thousand and eighty every month ; five hundred and ninety-six millions every year, the actual distance which the earth describes in its annual orbit; and even *this* is not all, for the rotary motion of our planet would involve another movement of the spirit, in the circular line of the surrounding atmosphere, at the immense velocity of twenty-four thousand eight hundred and forty miles every twenty-four hours.

What a marvelous sight it would be, were we permitted to look out through the eyes of the soul, and see the one hundred thousand persons, who depart from the earth every day in death, flying through space in the chase for life, and for the purpose of remaining near the mother world, and the dear friends left behind.

Nay! such thoughts are preposterous. As there is a life to succeed our present form of existence, so sure is that life limited to the regions of the aerial ocean above our heads, at all events temporarily, and so sure are the beings who dwell therein, existing in some form well adapted to the refined medium which is their home. They stand upon no solid basis, but like the clouds which flee before the winds, they are probably subject to restrictions, in their altitudinal range, and float, rather than walk, above the conflicting powers which pertain to the mundane sphere.

They are silent, because the interests of the earth and heaven require their silence. They are unseen because nature has so decided. But it is evident, that, in time, we shall be able to gain a more perfect knowledge of Spirit-life; for, as mankind become wiser, they will inevitably discern the true relation which exists between matter and spirit, between cause and effect, and comprehend the action, if not the nature, of the unswerving laws, which establish the identity and control the destiny of the immortal soul.

When we contemplate the subject of a future life, we should be extremely shy of the acceptance of accommodating theories, should be wary in our research and reason, and never permit ourselves to be happified, so to speak, by flattery or the standard opinions of designing and artful thinkers. Even our love for the departed should not blind our perception, as against the interest of truth, nor cause us to receive an hypothesis, simply because it bears a genuine appearance or is hopefully gratifying.

Mankind have sought refuge in a thousand varying theories, in strange and inadmissible views, concerning the event of death and the great hereafter. Men have mourned and prayed, while women have sighed and wept over a fear of the grave, and the want of safety of the soul, on account of individual faults and defects.

Theology, serving humanity in the prerequisites of its own faith and ceremonials, has, in good part, banished from the domain of its literature and teachings, nearly every idea of freedom of thought or personal responsibility, presuming to ignore the deductions arising from scientific inquiry, as well as the better rules of logical antithesis employed in debate. The great question of a future life is, in popular theology, merely one of conjecture, of inference, of fashionable twaddle. It is not considered as one of the certainties and successes of nature—as fundamentally true, or as an inevitable gift of the organic laws of creation, but is the unsettled object of a Divine mysteriousness, which is as captious as it is uncertain.

The visions of the imagination have supplanted the actual in reflection. The common mind has not been able to understand or appreciate the value of comparative or critical evidence. The *old* has been revered instead of the *new*. The superstitious systems of the past have been received and fostered, through ignorance, selfish interest, and a vaunted conservation, without regard to the better demands of the human mind.

The principle of reason is seldom allowed to fashion the adjuncts of power in the sphere of ecclesiastical action. It is only where science is brought to our aid, or gives us the benefit of her willing analyzations, it is only when mathematics assail the citadels of impertinent bigotry and putrescent religions, that we come to distinguish between right and wrong, between truth and amiable falsehood, between the evidences which are self-supporting and the shams and fictions of time-honored lore and logic.

The rationalistic philosophy of Spiritualism provides means for the demonstration of its principles. It adopts measures whereby we are enabled to free ourselves from religious and intellectual mistakes and blunders, from the foibles, fallacies, deceits and imperfections which pertain to credulity and human confidence.

The knowledge that we are to inherit a superterrestrial condition of being, as a result of the outworking sentence of Infinite law—that life is no specialty, but the gift of Divine wisdom, and eternally self-maintaining ; the idea that we may all comprehend, in a satisfactory degree, the nature of that life which we are to accept beyond the grave, the thought that we can contemplate it as a verity and understand it as a reality, that we can conceive of it by reflection, and reach it through analogy, perception, mental analysis, and methodical communion with the departed, are not only so many evidences of our superior success—the success of an enlightened Spiritualism—but, as well, a gauge for the relief of the world, from its false notions, time-abiding errors, and deeply channeled religious beliefs.

It is one of the wise and beneficent purposes of the Supreme Ruler of nature, that we are to live and receive the schooling of "eternal experience," that we are to rise from the surface of the earth, when the spirit is separated from the physical body, in the event of death, and reside in more congenial and less conflicting relationships of being. It is nature's qualification that the human spirit is substance, that it is organically formed, and like all other forms, has its origin in the aggregation or growth of sympathetic atoms, which combine under the most inscrutable chemical processes.

It is not only evident that mental principles are

derived from the spirit of matter, in good part, but it is quite as certain that their centralized association in the conscious, organic mind, is supported and maintained, in our present state of being, through incessantly replenishing action.

The vital energy of life is constantly renewed from two sources ; the food of which we partake and the atmosphere which we inhale. Of the substance and the essence thus appropriated to our use, the immortal spirit is formed and perfected in its. organic and ethereal nature. Thus, it is more than probable, that when the spirit abandons its casket of clay, and rises to reside in more exalted realms of life, it is still likely to remain dependent upon congenial atmospheric support, and can not fly away into any and all positions, situations and regions, to satisfy its capricious desires and ambitions.

As well might we expect to find a South-sea Islander upon the snow-clad elevations of Mount Washington, there to remain, as an earth-born spirit beyond the awful, illimitable confines of the Milky-way. As well might we contemplate a sudden transfer of the populations of Asia to some broad continent of the western world, as to anticipate the meeting of earth's immortal hosts in some far off, indefinite realm of the heavens.* The destiny of all races and nations is the. same in import and design. We are provided with a spirit-home near our present place of abode, if at all, and that, no doubt, for many centuries. The

---

* The author would not be understood as asserting that spirits can not pass over the inter-planetary spaces, or that they may not eventually live in space.

earth's aerial ocean must be a surging sea of Life. The communities of the air must be far more numerous than those of the planetary sphere. Unseen billions of immortal souls must congregate in watchful attendance over us, guiding and guarding the interests of human households.

Nature is, indeed, a Divine Arbitrator, and forbids confusion as much as she cherishes the worthy objects of place, use and consistency. There is no fallaciousness of purpose in the economy of creation. Every living thing is governed by fixed and unchangeable laws—is hampered and restricted, to limits wisely determined by the accessory action of matter and its refined life. The stars weave and turn in their distant orbits, the planets roll and tumble through space, each being held to its place and position, by a binding obligation which no power can molest or destroy, the all-controlling will of the Omnipotent mind.

The fleecy comets traverse the open vista of the sky, through distances absolutely inconceivable, secreting themselves from our vision for hundreds and thousands of years, when, with that regularity which is ever affixed to the agencies of the Divine Spirit, they return to our view, submissively yielding to that influence which is held over them, as orbs of one common origin and family.

The great belt which spans the heavens and sparkles with the glowing light of countless spheres, is forever steadfast in its suspended location. The wandering suns of immensity, as well as the multiplied atoms of which their bulky forms are composed, are bound down by the rigid power of Supreme command, ever yielding to established laws, which holds them to their place and destiny.

Wherefore, are we to suppose, that the liberated soul or spirit is wholly its own dictator, being free from the hampering influence of Divine control, free to roam at large without the interposition of a barrier to its own fancies and desires, when all other things, of which we have any knowledge, are held down by the force of magnetic centralization in form and substance.

It is not true! While the released soul may find a broader region, a wider dominion wherein to dwell, than was accorded to its experience while a resident upon the planetary world, it may not be presumed that its life is not overborne by the action of unalterable principles, or that it can will itself into a selfish monopoly of time, place, and space.

Thus it is self-evident, that we are to live in the future, as beings of substantial form, of aerial existence, of conditioned happiness and restrained desires, if nature's promises are true. Instead of wading, as we do at present, at the bottom of a vast ocean of atmospheric fluids, to maintain life by contact with natural objects and things, we shall drop off the outward covering, the body of flesh and bone, and rise to live in the "sea of air" as creatures of immortal mould.

THE ONLY HOPE.

***

A MESSAGE FROM THE INNER LIFE.

***

The remarkable communication which is herewith presented, concerning the experience of a brother in Spirit-life, was imparted to my interior hearing in the early part of the winter of 1874. Its transmission required seven different sittings, which occupied, in all, some twenty evening hours. It was written nearly as herein given, the many new and singular words which it contains, receiving their orthographical construction from my own idea of plain spelling and utterance, rather than from their accurate enunciation as I heard them spoken—often hastily—by the spirit.

To the reader we offer this message as one of the many wonderful evidences which tend to establish the reality of an immortal state of existence, and as an expression of the singular processes of mental effort and activity which pertain to educational research and training in that soul-realm toward which we are all tending, and of which, at best, in this world, we can form but a very imperfect conception.

BROTHER'S MESSAGE.

"When I first came to this world of beauty and refinement, my brother, I was not only surprised and delighted, but, as you would say, I was 'favorably disappointed;' for, having departed from the earth in that inaptitude of mind, which is so characteristic of outward life, I was overjoyed to realize the truth of my former belief in a 'future state of existence,' and in experiencing a condition of being, so very different, yet, withal, so much more desirable and pleasant than I had anticipated.

"When I had been but seven months with my beloved sister Caroline, whose care was given to bless my early realizations in this life, I could look back, and view my past relation to earthly interests with ample knowledge of the consequences which it involved. I found that existence was not what I had supposed it to be. I discovered that it was not necessary to be *qualified* in order to reach the 'immortal realm' in safety. Looking to nature I could readily understand, that the 'gift of being,' was conferred upon man as a result of the action of unswerving laws. I could discern the instrumentality which had produced and supported my existence upon earth, and, in all things, I found myself not less dependent upon the charity of omniscient purpose here.

"As I became a spirit, so was I delighted with the consciousness of 'life immortal;' and although my individual ideas and opinions were wholly derived from the imperfect elements of

education and contemplation, which I had realized and enjoyed as a result of personal desire
and effort upon earth, still I lost no time in my
endeavor to attain to that more gratifying condition, in knowledge, and consequent happiness,
which is ever to be found among the dwellers in
the *Akseolza** of the Spirit-land.

"When the day of my departure from my
earthly home arrived, I was quite unconscious of
the approach of the marvelous and important
change which it was to be mine to experience. I
had, it is true, long suffered from bodily disease and weakness, and had lived in remote an-
ticipation, if not fear, of the ever unwelcome event
of death. In my most serious meditations, however, I had not believed the final change to be so
near, neither had I the remotest idea of the effect
of physical dissolution in renewing the privilege
of life in the immortal world.

"The morning of my release from the thralldom
of the gross material body which I had worn, I
was enjoying an ordinarily comfortable state of
mind, little thinking that another hour or two
would close my career as an earth-bound spirit,
or that I should be restored to life, in this, to
you, 'unseen sphere of existence.'

"When the sad moment arrived—which you so
well remember, my dear brother—and which took
me from you so suddenly, as the result of stran-
gulation,† I was thrown into the deepest state of

---

* The common home of the newly arisen spirit populations which emanate from the earth.

† From a rupture of the pulmonary artery.

mental anxiety and anguish, realizing all the emotions of sadness, doubt and despair.

"In two minutes from the time I became aware of the presence or inflowing of blood into the air passages of my left lung, I was deprived of all consciousness, and not a sensation of any kind molested my thoughts or disturbed my slumbering faculties.*

"The 'principle of will,' which is fundamental to all life, is either self-active in awakening the senses of the new-born spirit to consciousness, or, otherwise, is psychologically influential in arousing the elements of the spiritual organization to newness of being. Thus the process of transformation is established, and in due time the immortal mind is cut away from all connection with the physical form and the relationships which pertain to the material world.

"I was personally unmindful of the change which was being effected in my condition, for something near an hour and thirty minutes. At the expiration of this period, and at the option of a guardian *Izo*,† I was released from the mortal body, wherein I had lived for so many years,‡ and in company with a number of friends, in Spirit-

---

* My brother was sitting up in bed taking his morning's repast from a salver, which had just been placed before him by my mother, the other members of our family being at breakfast in an adjoining room. He had been eating but a few moments when suddenly he cried out, "I am bleeding to death," and these were his last words, as he sunk back upon his pillow and expired.

† A watchful and attentive spirit. Sometimes an *accoucheur*, or one who attends upon the resurrection of the dead.

‡ Nearly twenty-one.

life, I was conveyed to the heights of *Kareansa*,* where for a season I was made comfortable by the kindly attentions of my beloved sisters.

"While journeying with those who had come to aid me—in what constituted the needful requirements developed by my translation—from the place where my prostrate earthly body lay, to our dear sisters' home on the celestial plain of *Monomanilla*,† I was constantly thinking of the causes involved in the change which I had realized. Being, as yet, unacquainted with the *Izo*, who seemed to take the greatest immediate interest in my comfort and welfare, and feeling somewhat timid, owing to the newness of my situation, I did not, at first, venture to say anything ; but at length, borrowing courage from my curiosity, I reluctantly inquired :

"'Who art thou, that with my beloved sister Caroline, hath so far considered my needs as to come to earth and escort me to my new home whither thou art going ?'

"This inquiry was prompted by my feelings. I realized a sorrowful objection to, and could not see the propriety of being so soon compelled to depart from my earthly home, and the dear friends whom I was obliged to leave behind. My sister smiled as she observed my uneasiness, while the robust *Izo*, likewise perceiving my anxiety, and being at the moment in seeming of fraternal, if not humorous thought, kindly replied :

"'We are only delegated to accompany thee to

---

* Place of supine joy.
† A peopled stratum in aerial regions.

a sister *Wahlon*,* where care and comfort are in reserve to meet the demands of thy necessities.'

"I was now quite satisfied, and when I arrived at the place where my dear sisters were living, in all the joy and happiness of their interesting and exalted life, I was not only well cared for, but my spirit sisters both wept when in their heart-felt gratitude they contemplated my release from years of physical suffering.

"I had not been long in the enjoyment of my repose, when feeling improved in my condition, and thinking, one evening, that I should like to know something concerning the *Imon*,† whom I could see moving in various directions along the great plain of *Monomanilla*, I remarked to sister Caroline, with whom I was at the time in conversation, thus:

"'May I journey to where the many *Imo* live, whom we can see from our *Wahlon* moving to and fro in the azure heights over *Tamino*?'‡

"Speaking thoughtfully, she answered and said:

"'It is not best, my dear brother, for you to go there alone, as the *Poase* § are only too gracious to be inconvenienced by the solicitations of a rising *Kamaon*.‖ When I can well resign my many duties in the *Savizana*,¶ or, at home, as you would say, I shall be pleased to accompany you

---

* A temporary home where sorrow is abated.
† Observers. A celestial people.
‡ An intermediate sphere.
§ Wise possessors, in a mental sense.
‖ One restless in thought.
¶ The guardian's council station or realm.

thither ; and we can then, not only enjoy ourselves temporarily, but may be benefited by a
conference with these truly noble people—learning something in regard to their refined manners
and superior educational attainments.'

"Until the time to which I here refer, it had
not been my pleasure to leave my sister Caroline's
presence.   I really had not found a moment when
I could, for the very good reason, that my new
life had to be maintained in quietness and repose
for several weeks after I became a spirit ; and although my lameness—which was the cause of my
greatest misery upon earth—was now entirely re-
moved,* I discovered that to conform to the circumstances of my new situation, was not so easy
a task as might be inferred without experience.

"After a time, and upon a favorable occasion,
I went with sister to visit the *Imon* in whom I had
become so much interested, and who sojourn upon the elysian plain of *Monomanilla* far to the
westward of her aerial home.   I was highly delighted with the pure and pleasant method of
immersed conversation employed by them, when
speaking with each other, or with those who visit
them.   I was also pleased to observe the graceful
make-up and beauty of their many-colored *Sha-
netokas* or 'garments of honor,' and in their
charming *Tolekas* I found something to interest
my curiosity as well as to surprise and instruct
my mind.   The *Toleka* is given or kept to ap-
pease the misfortunes of the understanding.   These

---

* My brother was lame for upwards of three years with a
scrofulous cancer near the left knee-joint. It brought on
consumption, and eventually caused his death.

variable 'tokens' or 'toys of memory,' are but the 'symbols of thought' subordinated to the interests of spirit elevation, and are made an offering to the soul in its discernment of future blessedness.

"Contemplating the happiness which those around me seemed to enjoy—realizing something of the beauty and perfection represented in the many new and singular objects which I beheld, I could not resist the impulse of a spontaneous desire, which came welling up from within my consciousness, to make my delight known; and so I remarked to a *Zanamo* who had been long a resident on the *Mase**** in this sphere, that if he would receive and instruct me, I would remain with and subserve his recommendations.

"Looking at me for a moment with a pleasant yet penetrating gaze he musingly replied:

"'Will you be composed in mind'—he observed that I was inclined to irritability of thought —'and endeavor to be kind and considerate?'

"'Yes,' I answered, 'I will try and follow every good example and accept all worthy counsel.'

"Again placing his eyes upon me with steadfast look, as if entertaining a doubt in regard to the sincerity of my words, he quietly remarked:

"'Would you object to being consigned to our *Losao*, for a period, to study the 'mein' in the opportunities and advantages of being?'

"The import of this question and the peculiar

---

* The *Mase* appears to be a special home or location where the wise *Zanamo* live. They are discreet and stubborn thinkers.

manner in which it was expressed—which can only be known to a spirit—were to me strongly indicative of distrust, for the *Losao* is a place of correction for all manner of mental defects or temperamental imperfections, and so I said :

" 'Would you be pleased to take and try me ?'

"Seeing the readiness with which I answered, yet feeling more inclined to question me than accommodate my over-anxious desires, he finally replied :

" 'The truth is, you are so young in spirit, that I can not wisely comply with your request ; moreover, your kind, elder sister here, is blessed with much alacrity and good-will in this life, and it is well for you to abide with her.'

" 'I was now convinced that the chances for my remaining with the *Zanamo*, or 'wise and gifted student of nature,' were decidedly remote, and as my sister smiled at my ambition, I said, with a feeling of mortification and disappointment :

" 'I confess that my knowledge in regard to what it is best to do, is somewhat deficient, my dear Caroline, but I am not altogether hopeless, and, at your pleasure, I am quite satisfied to remain on the *Conseento** in our realm.'

"We were engaged in observing the various peculiarities represented in the habits, manners and occupations of the spirits who dwell on the far-spreading *Monomanilla*, and were overjoyed by our happy experiences, when thinking that we had been absent quite long enough, we turned to

---

* Con-se-en-to, a section of the Ak-se-al-za, to which reference has been made.

make our way toward the place of sister's residence.

"In journeying homeward, so to speak, we were invited to visit the celestial plaza of *Inza Konwehn*, a place where good souls become exalted in wisdom, and where the well-inclined are chosen under an obligation to improve. This pleasant place of learning and progress is occupied by the thoughtful and righteous spirits of many nations. It was founded in honor of *Konwehn*, a good and noble soul, who always reposed the fullest confidence in the 'wise precepts' of 'celestial gatherings,' as a means for the promotion of moral and intellectual good.

"All places of learning or of 'wise council,' are, in this life, only held to occupancy so long as they are made subservient to the purposes of instruction, or the inculcation of useful and redemptory precepts. When they are no longer thus used they become the common inheritance of the spirit *Lanivo*, or 'monitors from below.'

"It is not our privilege to hold and dispose of property as is the custom upon earth. We are only privileged to restore that which nature gave for our comfort. We are free from all obligations which do not come within the bearing of *mental compensation*.

"Thus you will observe that to become a resident of the Spirit-world, is to be deprived of all wealth, save that which comes from the action, growth and elevation of the mind, and there is no way to change this mandate of Infinite Wisdom.

"When we were living on the far-extending plain of *Monomanilla*, where I received my first

lesson in the true knowledge of life—from one of
the most considerate preceptors with whom I have
ever met, a spirit *Imo*, of much good-will and
happy purpose of mind, ever ready and willing
to aid the well-intended desires of those who associate together in the 'councils of the blest'—I
was not called Jacob, as upon earth, but instead
thereof I received the somewhat singular name
of *Somioni*, which refers to 'personal hope' as
it pertains to existence in the 'future.' We say
the 'only hope,' as applied to the individual, is
an evidence or a promise of forthcoming knowledge and wisdom, the specific expression of which
is given in the 'life.' This title is really of but
temporary use, and is only applied to the *Vauso*,
or 'anxious students,' who are urged by feelings
of deep solicitude to seek the benefits of personal
improvement.

" When upon a time I visited the *Vzoni* of the
Only Hope, where all spirit attendants are first
instructed in the ways of immortal life, the *Zanza*
or principle teacher, whose name was *Orobine*—he
being then 'master in council' of the *Foni*, a
body of young and impatient students—very
pleasantly remarked to me :

" ' Would you like to come and remain for a
season with our *Varivodo*,* and see if you can
make yourself useful and happy ? Perhaps you
may become more joyous and hopeful, in regard
to the Divine Ordinations, as they relate to life
and the future, by so doing.'

" Meditating for a moment I earnestly answered
and said :

---

* Spirits of all shades of mind in advancement.

"'I shall not only be pleased to conform to your 'desire,' but shall, as well, be thankful to be made acquainted with your anticipations of hope.'

"Perceiving my thoughts and understanding my wishes, he again very calmly remarked:

"'When there is an opening in the *Vessavi** of the Only Hope, it shall be yours to enjoy.'

"I waited with patience for many months before I received permission to engage in the duties incumbent upon a student of this wonderful place of learning. When, however, I was admitted to the benefits and opportunities therein presented, I was soon employed in the most earnest thought and study, being at once guided by a *Kuao*,† through the 'designs of observation,' a most marvelous lesson in this life.

"The way I happened to go to the Only Hope for instruction, was this: Sister Caroline had several times accompanied me and sister Jennett thither, and I had become deeply interested in the methods of mind-culture therein pursued. I could observe, as I thought, that they were strictly in accordance with the best interests of mental well-being, and consequently I determined to patronize the fine advantages thus to be secured.

"It was not understood by me, however, at that time, that it was a difficult task to accomplish the objects of scholarship in that remarkable place of instruction; but I soon discovered that I was greatly mistaken, for the *Shanelon*, or portion of the Only Hope where the students are

---

* First department. Renewal of mind.
† One accurate in perception. A teacher.

vivacious and unsubdued, is really a most troublesome place in which to receive the benefits of
education ; and this is the more so, since the influence of discipline sought to be made effective
in the suppression of levity and various other
forms of disorder, is really somewhat difficult to
establish, even though managed by the strongest
powers of foresight and wisdom.

"Notwithstanding all this, however, the course
of rudimentary studies therein pursued, is enjoy-
able as well as ennobling, and those who are willing to conform to the rules and requirements
which are connected therewith, never fail of being
advanced in knowledge or benefited in mind.

"There are altogether some fourteen hundred
teachers in this 'aerial, mental infirmary,' and
they are an earnest and dutiful vanguard of mind,
ever ready to give the hand of fellowship to anxious seekers after truth, and in that, to bestow
upon them, the gracious gifts and symbols of
thought which are used—with caution and adaptation—to educate the young *Matimo*.

"The manner in which these figurative gifts are
used, as a source of expediency, in training the
mental spheres—or, as you would say, faculties
—to conditions of higher harmony and more responsible action, is in a bestowal in doubtful meta-
phor of thought. The *Zanza* addressing a member of his *Foni* or class, *per se*, perhaps, inquires
if he will not accept a beautiful *Toleka*, which is,
at the same time, held up before the mind, for observation.

"If the student is a new comer, and is not cir-
cumspect in comprehension, he will not be likely

to ask any questions, but simply saying: 'I am happy to be so comforted,' or something to that effect; he is allowed to receive it, being thus far, wholly uninstructed as to the chastening signification, or secret meaning represented by the 'token.'

"When the gift has been accepted, the teacher, or a *Lataon*—one who educates by perplexing methods—inquires of the student as to the reason of his accepting it.

"To this the answer—more than likely given in haste or indiscretion—is to the effect, 'that it looked so attractive, or appeared so inviting,' or otherwise, 'I thought you gave it out of a comforting consideration.'

"To this the preceptor would again very quietly reply:

"'The *Toleka*, which you hold, I fear, is not for thee, for only those who can comprehend its *use* and *real signification* can profitably retain it as their own.'

"To this the thought-seeking and industrious *Matimo* might, with propriety, again respond:

"'I was not informed that there were reserved conditions attached to the acceptance of the *Toleka*.'

"This remark might, perhaps, be regarded as indicative of a superficial perception, hence the *Lataon* would be likely to remark:

"'I presume you have not given the subject, symbolized by the 'token,' that close attention which it deserves. There is a redemptory signification embodied in the form and make-up of the *Toleka*, which those only who are discerning, can

readily understand. Music, you know, has two
forms : that which is accordant and that which is
discordant. The first promotes pleasure and happiness, the latter engenders misery and ill feeling.
The same rule holds good in regard to thought,
knowledge or judgment. There is a choice in the
'objects of the mind' as there is a design in the
wisdom of their arrangement. True intellectual
worth is an inestimable treasure, and can only be
secured through the exercise of the most free and
accurate perception and reflection. Now, as a
student in the *Vessavi* of the Only Hope, let me
further recommend to your consideration, the
form, use and purpose, designed to be conveyed
by the beautiful symbol which you hold, and
which you are still permitted to retain.'

"Thus it is that by gradual prompting, that by
newly-awakened curiosity, that by kindly-given
advice and well-applied influence, the mind of the
seeker after knowledge is aroused to energy—is
invited to recognize habits of industry, and to
heed the whisperings of a devoted spirit, while
trying to search out the hidden meaning of things.

"The object of the *Toleka*, or the reserved signification which it is intended to represent, is
sooner or later disclosed to the wisdom faculties
of the searcher after truth, and the mind is, hence,
improved by its investigations and efforts.

"When first asked if I would be pleased to accept a *Toleka*—which, in this instance, represented *amiability*—I said, with a doubtful air of
jocularity and caution :

"'I fear I am not sufficiently adroit in thought
to discover its hidden meaning.'

" The beautiful *Zanzaress*—an angel of mercy
—who was attending upon our *Foni*, and whose
name was *Mereonta*, perceiving my timidity and
facetious inclination, at once interested herself by
saying:

" 'The *Toleka* is intended for, and is employed
as an aid to the mind, in its effort to gain une-
quivocal intelligence and wisdom. It is desirable
that, at times, we should turn our attention to the
many lessons which tend to strengthen thought—
that we may become 'masters in wise decision.'
To this end, the true import of the *Toleka* is
given in 'judgments,' which correct or establish,
in the understanding, the real value as well as
virtue of all conclusions, ability or pre-determined
purpose.'

"As a result of the explanations and kindly
advice given by our pleasant preceptress, I was
induced to accept the symbolic token which she
presented, with a view to the discovery of its hidden meaning, and the *uses* which that meaning
implied.

"When I had learned my first lesson I was
greatly delighted, in view of having escaped without making any serious mistakes, as is often the
case with the unexperienced *Matimo*. When,
however, I was called upon to perform the task
involved in my second lesson, which consisted of
the conception and delivery of a short soliloquy
on the *Pantomena* of mind, or 'the characteristics of mental action,' I was so unfortunate as to
be unable to properly present the subject ; and I
was in as much mortification, at the result of my
effort, as on the previous occasion I had been

made glad by my success. Our good and consid-·erate preceptress, observing my restlessness and anxiety, approached me with a smile of satisfaction upon her face, when in a mood of petulance, and with an air of subdued consequence I ventured to ask :

"'May I not receive your generous support in my effort to obtain an insight into the mystery of my lessons ?'

"To this she rather evasively, though properly, replied :

"'If you will consider your own needs, reflect upon your own investigations, or, in other words, help yourself more freely, it shall be my pleasure to give you aid in instruction.'

"Thus, while I was not without generous assistance from the wise and gifted *Mereonta*, I was made to feel a personal responsibility, which, although one that I realized for some time, as a heavy burden to bear, I eventually discovered was the true source of my joy and success, in the pursuit of my studies.

"By a singular arrangement, and for a reason, to me, for a period unknown—it being a privilege belonging to the *Zekkaron*,* not permitted to be understood—I was only in the first-class of enlightened *Mivesoes*, who are said to enjoy the 'only hope,' yet, with restricted perception, especially as to the 'coming time;' hence the *Alloni*, or more advanced students, were alone able— owing to their improved condition in mental training—to say that the classes in our *Komonso*, or

---

* A Council-place where teacher and educators meet.

department, as you would say, were comprehensively in the light of 'present hope;' and this, as I afterwards discerned, was true, for, by the 'inward guide,' which is ever personal to the individual in exalting and fixing the status of manhood, so to speak, in our life, they were justly entitled to that conclusion.

"When I had eventually mastered the many lessons administered to the students of the *Vessavi*, which required considerable time and close attention to the objects of patient research and thought, I could see that the 'only hope' pertained to the 'future;' for, by an awakening sense of insight into the *Psito** of 'eternal distress and distrust,' and the relationships compelled through the law of action, I could readily discern that, in accepting the marvelous 'gospel of confidence,' as established by our *Teeno* or 'wise confessors,' I was obliged to forego that joy and happiness in the consciousness of life, which I had supposed that I realized and possessed; and was alone permitted to accept that personal promotion, which is accorded to the mind, as the result of a laudable ambition and desire, or otherwise, in its earnest search for that knowledge which is ever reliable and true.

"Thus you will not hesitate to accept the conclusion, my brother, that the course pursued in training the minds of the newly initiated students of the Only Hope, while it is well calculated to undo our pre-added inclinations, imperfections and faults, is, at the same time, an effectual

---

* A perception of the prevarication of Infinite operations and power.

source of personal improvement, intellectual
growth and gain.

"When I had so far advanced as to take the
next step in my educational progress, I was not
only better prepared to drink in the sublime lessons of 'hope,' in connection with the 'wise precepts' of our *Hiatimo*,* but I was ready to be
continued to the 'higher light' of 'wise intentions,' which could only have been received in a
somewhat advanced stage of mental prepared-
ness.

"Thus you will perceive that in our life it is
first necessary to learn 'hope,' next the 'objects
of hope,' then the 'precepts of wise counsel,' after that, 'the gospel of confidence,' then, and
lastly, 'the law of operative design,' in its application to 'entrusted power.'

"When I had attained to that condition of
mental self-reliance, which is so essential to success in obtaining instruction in the 'precepts of
wisdom,' as taught in the *Seona* of the Only
Hope, I was then much better prepared to apply
such precepts to advantage in my experience in
this life.

"The great benefit derived from our processes
of mental training, consists in the permanency of
the accordant relations thereby established in the
'spheres of the mind.' The soul or will, which
is centered in a union of the senses, becomes
stronger, and the mind is rendered mature in
judgment and wisdom, by our methods. This
truth can only be realized by those who have re-

---

* A class of gifted thinkers and reasoners.

ceived the advantages which are thus to be obtained, for the reason, that when a person first enters our realm from the earth, the inequalities of the mind are almost sure to promote impulsive action and thought, and the new comer is, as you would define it, 'impelled by motives of anxiety.'

"When I was in the aerial offings of *Moino*,* in the sedate classes of the 'Hope of *Ormoti*,'† I was not, as now, in the light of 'continuous receptivity of thought,' but otherwise, in 'the decisions of justice,' which combines propriety of thought with prudence in the announcement of our opinions; which virtually unites the *desire* to fathom the mysteries of the 'Divine Life,' with the *opportunity;* which associates the willingness to *know* with the wished-for *object;* which signifies, in a plainer sense, the interests of the 'Divine government' of 'Divine activity' and 'motive,' as observed throughout all nature.

"In this degree of educational progress we are restrained to silence, and even when the full graduating students of the *Kornawon*‡ depart from the West *Arito*§ of the Only Hope, to enter the *Vistena*‖ of life, we remain, as a spirit fraternity, in a subdued and quiet state of reflection, uttering not a single word, what though, with some of the ambling *Parroti*,¶ we may have been for a long time associated in heart and nearness

---

* A place of celestial fellowship.
† A distinction in thought advanced by one Or-mo-ti.
‡ The graduating department of the Only Hope.
§ Departing avenue.
‖ Open, broad sphere.
¶ Wise patients.

together. This action is based upon the idea that while the spirit remains unperfected, or the mind fosters a joy in 'isolated hope,' its 'familiar confidence' is bemoaned.

"When a spirit is going away to some remote or indefinite region of the universe, and past friendships are to be severed, or, when present relationships are to be broken, it is our custom to think, that unless we are able to perceive, that the parties thus separating, will again meet in the future of time, that it is unwise to say farewell; hence, when the *Parroti* depart from the *Kornawon*, our *Tomonto*,* which includes many thousands of souls, weep in silence and in sadness at the thought of companionships severed by the dividing of the 'hosts of *Maonton*.'†

"It is, really, a sad sight, my brother, to see so many long-time friends wandering away through the heavens in every direction, no more to be united in the eager search for knowledge, no more to be associated in happy acquaintance or pastime together, in this life. Many of those who have been socially familiar, or who have become warmly attached to each other, through kindred nearness and sympathy, are here parted, never more, perhaps, to enjoy the pleasure of a restored intimacy—never more to meet.

"Like the fleeing of birds of passage, to some distant region—to some more congenial clime, is

---

* Those who are receiving new light.

† This word refers to the enlightened classes of the highest departments of the Only Hope, and is derived from the name of a distinguished Egyptian—Maontonosphor.

the departure of the *Parroti* from the West *Arito**
of the Only Hope.

"These egressions are marvelous to behold.
They take place at regular intervals, and not less
than from forty to seventy thousand souls, are
thus, betimes, liberated from the toils obligated by
association with the *Marnauns*,† and rise to receive the blessings of life, as provided for the en-
nobled spirit, in the broad sphere of *Sovonon*.‡

"The outgoing of the graduating classes, is
thus, as you will observe, a most wonderful sight
to look upon. By comparison, it reminds one of
the egress of a vast swarm of bees, as they depart
from the parent hive; yet, there is this difference,
the bees rise and cling together, the *Amano* dis-
solve and part.

"When the mind is once established in that
wisdom which is only to be gained by centuries
of observation, toil and study; or, in other words,
when the mind becomes fully developed in all of
its functions, powers and attributes, then the discernment of the sublime mysteries involved in the
study of 'Divine Engineering' becomes the highest and holiest object of mental ambition, and
the spirit, journeying through the illimitable
avenues of space, perceives and learns of the nature of the Infinite plan and purpose.

"To spirits thus wise, there is no longer any
doubt, uncertainty, hopelessness, distress or anxiety in regard to the 'future,' for, with such, there
is no 'coming time,' as through the instrument-

---

* Vestibule of egress from the *Kornawon*.
† Immortals in close proximity to the earth.
‡ A realm of exalted life and happiness.

ality of *will*, mental telegraphing is effected, and distance—by the instantaneous transmission of thought to very remote regions—is annulled, thus virtually annihilating all idea of time and space.*

"When I was in the final degree as a graduating student of the Only Hope, having been many month's engaged in acquiring the desirable lessons which are given, and that only in the 'council of present precepts,' in our *Rotaon Inswan* of 'wise designs,' I said to the kind-hearted *Zanza, Minotosi*, who, at that time, presided over the department, that I should like to be relieved of the obligations which were imposed upon me as a result of my confinement to the 'select lessons' which I was then engaged in pursuing, and that, with his permission, I should be pleased to return for a season to my sisters' home, where I might receive temporary freedom from mental care and anxiety.

"Looking at me with a genial smile upon his face, he at once replied :

"'You may go when it is your pleasure.'

"After a brief period, and after such needful preparation as circumstances required, I took leave of my many companions, and journeyed

---

* It is somewhat difficult to convey a clear conception of the revealments of the spirit as given through influx of thought to the semi-entranced senses. The writer was enabled to realize, through "psychologic impression," much more, in this connection, than he feels competent to disclose, or, than language is capable of expressing. The "only hope" as an idea, seems to have been built upon a theory of mental progress, as adopted by a wise spirit whose name was *Fonewosto*. His theory was, that "hope" was fundamental to the ambition of the mind, and led to knowledge, knowledge to understanding, and understanding to wisdom.

without delay to my sisters' home, where I was made glad by the welcome which I received. Indeed, the heart-felt expressions of a sister's love, were a source of joy and consolation to reward me for the many months of arduous devotion to study, which I had—in part unwillingly—endured; and to make my 'only hope,' which had already partaken of 'despair' and 'sorrow,' a blessing to me before unknown.

"When I had at length safely returned to sister Caroline's sight-commanding, aerial *Jottan*,* which is situated in view *of* the open plain of *Woanistah*,† I was in such ecstacies of delight, in consideration of my return, that for some time I was mostly inclined to remain in the quiet receipt of the many comforts which it was my beloved 'sister's wish that I should enjoy.

"I had been absent from Caroline's home for nearly eight months, and so overjoyed was she upon my arrival, that she gave expression to her happiness and satisfaction by saying:

"'Oh! dear brother, how delighted I am to think of your return. I hope that we may never be called upon to part from each other again.'

"'I hope not,' said I. 'it is much more agreeable to live in nearness together. While it is true that I have experienced much pleasure in my studies, and in the associations which I formed in the institution of the Only Hope, still I feel much happier in the society of my beloved sisters, and being nearer to my father's family upon the earth.'

* A guardian's place of observation.
† The spirit sphere of the aborigines of America.

"Sister Caroline had been long enough in the immortal world to realize something of the nature of the spirit-imparted lessons of 'Divine Despair,' which have a tendency to unite kindred hearts through a knowledge of the characteristics of 'universal change,' as sentenced in the infinite temple of the universe. Hence, she was more solicitous of my remaining near her, than I or sister Jennett was, of such close confinement.

"When, occasionally, I took a ramble out upon the broad *Zawane*—a lovely place, where many spirits seek comfort and consolation in peaceful retirement from mental cares, and where the wise *Navatah* dwell in silent, subdued happiness— then, pursuing me in my wanderings, she would chide me for the uneasiness and dissatisfaction which I often manifested.

"Once while listening to the sweet music of a flowing ethereal stratum called *Waneomla*, or 'methods in motion,' which meanders through the heavens like an earthly stream, sister Caroline came near me and said :

"'Wherefore, brother, do you come to observe *Waneomla* or pause to listen to its soft, inviting melody.'

"I looked at her for a moment and then, in a puzzle of mind, I replied :

"'The sweet sounds, which arise from its flow, are quite inviting, and moreover, it is very pleasant to look upon ; but whence does it come, dear sister, and whither does it go ?'

"Pausing for a moment, as if to gather her thoughts, she smilingly answered :

"'That is the mystery in which *Waneomla* is

involved. Its origin, although inferred, is not to
be found, while its termination is equally un-
traceable. *Waneomla* is, verily, a true symbol of
earth-life. It rises so gently from its predeter-
mined sources that its beginnings are unobserved.
When once it has attained form and motion, it
slowly advances in its onward course, giving expression to notes of murmuring music, while
sparkling in the light of its own activity. *Waneomla* moves along its chosen pathway—one wholly
determined by the make-up of its own elements
and power—and is soon lost in its absorbed and
hidden destiny. Do you not think that in *Waneomla* we have a good representation of life, as
known to man?'

"Thus, betimes, my dear sister * would amuse
herself by the suggestion of new ideas and
thoughts, by pointing to new objects of interest,
and by methods and in ways wholly at variance
with my experience. Sometimes she would speak
to me in words of consolation, then again she
would take delight in subduing my assumptions,
by showing me the way to humility in knowledge.

"When we were conversing together upon one
occasion, concerning the 'laws of life,' she very
significantly inquired :

"'What thinkest thou of the wisdom of men,
since thou hast observed their condition from our
realm?'

---

* My sister Caroline was the oldest of my father's family,
and died in August, 1837, hence, has been nearly forty years
in spirit-life.

"'Oh! bless me,' said I, 'I hardly know what to think.'

"'Well, then,' she remarked, observing the indefiniteness of my words, 'when I first came to this world I could not readily discern the capacity, peculiar inclinations, objects, purposes, desires or designs of mind, as I observed it enwrapt by the material substance of the physical brain in outward life. Three years subsequent to my entrance into this sphere and residence upon the *Marno** above my father's earthly dwelling, a friend came to me and said :

"'Caroline, would you like to journey with us —there were to be several in the party—in a tour of inspection around the mother world?'

"'Yes, indeed I would,' I answered, 'nothing could be more pleasant or better suited to my ambition.'

"'Then be soon prepared,' said the inquirer, as it is now our intention to journey toward the east in about one month, and we shall be happier for your presence and companionship in our travels.'

"'Yes,' said I, 'I will try and be ready. Accept my thanks for the kind offer which you have made me. It is really more than I could have expected.'

"'At the appointed time I was ready, and, together with fifteen companions, several of them having been long-time dwellers in this world—I withdrew from my local, aerial home — yet not without the appointment of a deputy to fulfill my guardian obligations—and journeyed on the *Sa-*

---

* The guardian spirits' plane of life.

lanse* toward the east. We passed over Montreal and the city of Quebec, thence above the Atlantic Ocean to Europe. We visited Ireland and England, looking down upon the city of London for three days and nights. From this point we journeyed to Constantinople, thence to the west coast of Africa, passing eastward from Liberia to the mid-waters of the Nile river, and onward over Arabia, Hindostan and China to the Phillippine Islands, from thence southerly to Guinea and New Holland, and from these islands eastward, once more, to the west coast of South America. After remaining over this continent for several weeks, we returned by the way of Columbia, Gautimala and Mexico to the east, to our respective homes, on the *Marno*, and our journey was at an end.

"We were absent on the *Salanse*, in this journey, just ninety days. During that time we had visited the principal nations existing upon the face of the earth, we had stood above the largest cities upon its surface, and had become impressed with the motives, feelings and interests which prompted men to action, which influenced them in their dealings with each other, which led to distress as well as happiness in the common concerns of life.

"Sister now paused for a moment as if in deep reflection, when suddenly addressing me she remarked by way of inquiry:

"'Wouldst thou observe the torments of sorrow and suffering as it exists upon the terrestrial

---

* A much-followed line of observation over the circle of the earth, in elevated atmospheric regions.

world.   Divine Judgments are wrought in every human soul.   The pleasures of being are counterpoised by the miseries of existence.   What sayest thou, brother, wouldst thou go with me to observe and contemplate the nature of things?   Wouldst thou know of the wonderful features of animal life, of the strange characteristics of humankind, as they exist—as only a spirit may know them?'

"Sister said nothing more, and so I replied :

"'Well, Caroline, really it is not my pleasure to be made more miserable than I am, over the *secreted faults* of mortals, but if life requires that my knowledge should be made oppressive to the happiness which I enjoy, I suppose it were wiser to meet the issue—as I used to say—manfully, and stare fate boldly in the face.'

"'Yes,' she answered, 'that is what it becomes necessary for all immortals to realize, and although the lesson is a sad one, it brings its reward, by conferring upon us a better understanding of the objects and purposes of the Great Divine Author, in the gift of consciousness and life. Ere long,' she continued, 'with your pleasure, we will seek the solicitudes, as well as the delights, which are to be met with in an aerial journey around the mother planet.'

"Thus it was that sister Caroline often took occasion to interest as well as instruct both Jennett and myself, soon after our arrival in the spirit home ; and thus we were gradually made familiar with the duties and obligations which a residence in our sphere of existence implies ; and sometime, my brother, when it is mutually agreeable, I will convey to you a narrative—in part—of what I saw in my first journey over the earth in the circle of *Salanse*.

"When I was in the Only Hope, which will forever add comfort and consolation to my heart, as my memory reverts to my experience there, I was not only in 'the best of spirits,' as you would say, but I was full of joy and confidence, in every good purpose, and this constantly increased with my educational advancement in that noble place of learning.

"The Only Hope was to me a balm which healed many personal imperfections. The more diversified ways of life were then and there made known to my understanding. The faults and follies which pertain to human existence were revealed in their true light. I soon comprehended the great issue to be decided in the outworking cause of creation. The lectures in 'wise council' which were given in the *Soloni* of 'present joy,' to the graduating classes, were to me a most happy source of instruction and knowledge. I was deeply interested in all that belonged to the explanations concerning the *Wonse*,* and I listened with pleasure to the tributes of praise which were extended to the just, the true, and the wise.

"In, and from all this, my brother, you may realize something in regard to my condition, something in regard to the anxiety which acted as a motive, prompting me to return again to you, that I might impart some intelligence in relation to my career as a spirit in the unseen realms of the immortal world.

---

* The *Wonse* belong to the lower grades of mind.

"When I was attending the lecture course, which is given in the *Soloni* of the Only Hope, where the motto is, 'the open judgments of the past,' or, 'nature divested of secrecy,' I was in the habit of remarking to those with whom I associated, that if my earthly brother could but once enjoy the delight of a look into this world, and could realize how I was situated, that it would be a source of enduring comfort and consolation to his bereaved spirit; and then on other occasions I would think of those loved ones whom I had left behind upon the earth, whose ever uppermost thoughts were directed heavenward in anxious supplication to know of my safety, and the conditions upon which my existence in the Spirit-world was made gratifying and permanent.

"When I first returned to the earth, in answer to your mental solicitation, I was not in the greatest ecstacy of hope as to the result of your appeal to be placed in conversational communion with us; and the accomplishment of securing to you the clairvoyant visions, which you now so much delight to enjoy, was not anticipated. When, however, after due investigation, we found your mental inclination in unison with our desire—through a love for the truth and long-continued affectionate regard for things of a spiritual import—we concluded that, with our aid, you might possibly serve some useful purpose in the world, and so we whispered in gentle words, by that impressional process which is confined to our method of *thought-communion*, that if you would absolve yourself from the harrassing circumstances of outward life, and place your sympathies in har-

mony of purpose with our intentions, we might
add to the sum of your personal happiness, by
enabling you to reveal many interesting facts and
truths concerning our life, and that, for the benefit of those who are anxious to consider the details
of new and oft-occurring phenomena, or who desire to comprehend the real relation existing between the outward world of humanity and the
inhabited spirit zones.

"Thus once more, dear brother, we are enabled
to speak again with each other, as when in childhood, thirty years agone, we lived and loved and
conversed together with familiar freedom, in the
'old home,' then made happy by the presence of
all the members of our father's household; and
now that we are again in conscious nearness of
being, and that you can realize that death *is not*,
but that 'life immortal' shines out from behind
the misty veil which separates your earth from
the Spirit-home, may it be your ever anxious wish
to so fashion your conduct, and mould your
worldly surroundings, so that you may be at
once, the recipient of useful impartations from
our realm of life, and one who can, in certainty,
give evidence that you can converse with us as we
converse together."

QUESTIONS AND ANSWERS.

The author has deemed it best to reply to the inquiries of certain friends and correspondents, through the medium of these pages, rather than to do so, separately, by letter. It is always a source of pleasure to ask as well as to answer questions, and it is, likewise, ever a mutual means of instruction and knowledge.

QUESTION.—F. G. W. asks: "How long do you think it will be before the indawning of the millennium? I have heard this matter talked of ever since I was a boy, but it don't appear to me to be any nearer now than it was then."

ANSWER:—Nature's laws are one and the same thing now and forever. Do not believe in a whimsical notion. The wisdom of man is not sufficiently *meek*, neither is his goodness sufficiently *strong* to bring about such a happy result. We may advance in learning, gain access to great thoughts, make progress in a hundred ways, still, difficulties and differences will exist, poison will continue to mingle its destructive elements with the "sweets of life," and the day will, probably, never come on earth, when the "Lion and the

Lamb" will lie down in peace together, notwithstanding the "say so" of a large class of religionists and others. Perhaps you may look upon this as a very sorrowful view of the subject. I do myself, but it is all that presents itself to my mind.

QUES.—H. B. T. inquires: "What is your opinion in regard to organization among Spiritualists?"

ANS.—I think, that in view of the fact that they are in good part deprived of the benefits of law and social respectability, as a disintegrated class of religionists—for Spiritualism is their religion—that they should organize for the purpose of more effectually aiding each other. I could not endorse the sectarianizing of Spiritualism in any bigoted or illiberal manner, but to organize for self-protection, or, to meet emergencies which may arise in the future, would seem to be wise and well.

QUES.—L. E. F. asks: "Why is it that you differ so materially with A. J. Davis and others, in regard to visions, and the freedom of the mind in the Clairvoyant state?"

ANS.—Oh! dear me, how it does distress some very good people because others—whom they would like to have enjoy a similarity of views—disagree. I have had my heart in brother Davis' writings ever since I can remember. I used to think that I could believe anything and everything which emanated from his pen. I have realized a marked change in regard to this matter. I now think that, of all men, he is, in some respects, the most mistaken. Some of the theories which he has advanced, are altogether untenable in the light of science. I can not say wherein brother Davis *is* or *is not* responsible for the views embodied in his writings. To me his philosophy is genial and pleasant, but not profound. He is wordy from the mouth of the spirit, and is wise, as he should be, in keeping his own counsels.

I differ with him as a thinker, as a writer, as a man. I scold a little sometimes to keep my children out of mischief. I don't suppose brother Davis was ever guilty of any such thing. He has visions, and I have visions. He says, as I understand him, that they are *objective;* I say they are *subjective.* He seldom engages in self-investigation or reasons, *a la critique*, upon the subject of his own experience. I look into my own realizations, consider and reflect upon them as well as upon my own thoughts. It seems to me as though brother Davis always labored to present the best side of philosophy to the mind. I want to see and understand both sides. If there is evil in Spiritualism, I want to expose it, placing it to the account of the realm to which it belongs. If there is good in it, I wish to enjoy it with the rest of the world.

I have suffered considerable from spirit control. I never can look upon it with happiness. Many others suffer in the same manner. I hear the dead speak, and I listen to their conversations in my normal condition of mind. I suppose Mr. Davis enjoys the same privilege. He calls it Clairaudiance, I call it sensative or "spirit hearing." Swedenborg was a recipient of the same gift, and so was Socrates. Swedenborg believed it was the Lord, at least, in some instances, so also,

in others, spirits and angels.   Socrates said he
was attended by a demon.   The probabilities are,
that Swedenborg was imperceptive, if not over-
confident, in regard to the real nature of his experience.   He was a great thinker, but his thoughts
were overborne by an *ignis fatus* of the fancy.
He was reflectively and theologically top-heavy.
He was good and kind, but dreamy and imagina-
tive in intellect.   Not so with Socrates.   He was
a self-poised philosopher of great mind.   He lived
on the even balance of reason, questioned the
studious and the learned without fear, making
free to affirm his belief in the idea, "that all truth
is susceptible of being comprehensively demonstrated."

Personally, I differ with Mr. Davis in regard to
the ability of the seer to see a spirit, as to its own
life—not as to a representation through visions.
I differ with him as to the import or suggestions
of nature in reference to the location of the Spirit-
world.   I differ with him as to the form of the
spirit.   I do not believe in "evil spirits" at all,
neither in "Diakka."   I think that spirits are,
mostly, wise and worthy, but that they impose
diabolisms upon us, to restrain our solicitude and
anxiety in regard to the things of the future, if
not, in some instances, to subdue our pretentions.

I am much inclined to think that the idea of
"seven spheres of existence," as taught by Mr.
Davis, and before him by Swedenborg, and before
both by ancient cabalistic writers, is a child of
the unfeigned imagination.   I think we are as
much mixed up in Spirit-life as we are here.   I
hardly know how I should get along, or what I

should do were it not for the many differences
which appear in all things. I love to contemplate
nature's variability. They learn the lesson of life
the most perfect, who fearlessly regard it in all of
its forms and phases. We differ with each other
because we can not help it. Our eyes are not
alike in color; our features are not of the same
shape; our motions and movements vary when
we walk. We feel and act according to our tem-
peraments, ability, and the nature of our surroundings. Who can say that we are not better
for our differences?

Ques.—J. K. makes this inquiry: "What is the present
condition of the moon? Is it inhabited by any living creatures, or does its surface present any form of vegetable
life?"

Ans.—Science, by means of the telescope and
other delicate instruments, has reduced the distance to the moon a thousand times, thus bringing
it optically within two hundred and fifty miles
of our stand-point of observation. The moon is
a satellite of rough and uneven surface, being,
evidently, full of mountains and hilly promi-
nences. The level plains look as though they
were surrounded by massive, high walls. As-
tronomers do not discover the presence of water
or air upon the moon. My Spirit Guide has said
to me, upon one or two occasions, that the moon
was the *dead body* of a once living sphere. That
its surface was once peopled by several species of
diminutive animals, like rats, but never by man.
Its vegetable productions were very limited, and
consisted principally of lichens, and a few varie-
ties of small plants, with patches of a kind of

grass, here and there, not over two inches high.
He said, likewise, that this state of things existed
about eighty-five thousand years ago, at a time
when the earth was in the flush of her wonderful
vegetable productions, and before man had appeared upon its surface. I was informed, likewise, that all worlds live and die like the vegetable and animal kingdoms to which they give rise ;
that the chill of death commenced at the poles
and receded toward the equatorial regions, that
when a world was dead, and all life had become
extinct upon its bosom, its distended atmosphere,
becoming refined by incessant action during long
ages, evaporated into space, leaving it destitute
of an aerial covering. Such is the present condition of the moon in all probability.

Ques.—Mr. H. Veeder, of Plattsburg, N. Y., writes: "Having been considerably interested in Confucius and his teachings for some years, I have gathered up such books, from
time to time, as I could concerning them. I recently pro-
cured your "Life and Moral Axioms of Confucius," and I
now wish to inquire of you concerning the 'Golden Rule.'
You give your version of it as follows; viz., Maxim 100: *Do
unto another what you would he should do unto you;* and
do not unto another what you would not should be done
unto you. *Thou needest but this law alone; it is the foun-
dation and principle of all the rest.*

"In Dr. Legges' translation we find it worded thus: 'What
I do not wish men to do to me, I also wish not to do to men.'
Then again: 'What you do not want done to yourself, do
not do to others.' Also: 'What you do not like done when
done to yourself, do not do to others.'

"You will see that in these translations there are no *positive precepts,* but rather *injunctions,* requiring us not to do
certain wrong things, but not telling us to do certain right
things, although the positive inference is clear enough.

"I know an Orthodox minister who has specifically asserted, in his pulpit, that the Golden Rule was never **given** until Christ gave it; all other analogous sayings **having** been merely *negative* utterance.

"In your version you construct a positive injunction and add a conclusion—*'Thou needest but this law alone.'*

"Now I wish to inquire, has 'Confucius' given the Golden Rule in a positive form—as Christ did? And further, does he give any similar conclusion to it?"

ANS.—In the phraseology given to the Golden Rule, as taught by Confucius, and interpreted by different authors, I have presented that form which seemed best to express the innate idea or doctrine designed to be conveyed. That Christ presented the maxim in a more positive light, or that he clothed it in more positive words than the great Chinese moralist did, there is no good reason for assuming. Christ said: "Therefore all things whatsoever ye would that men should do to you, do ye even so to them;" *this is the law and the prophets.* Another version reads thus: "In all things therefore that ye would that men should do unto you, do ye even so unto them, *for this is the law and the prophets.*" Then again: "In the things therefore that ye would that others should do to you, do ye unto them, for this is the law and the prophets."

The wording of any axiom or text, is, at the best, a very variable matter, and especially where these are translated from other languages, or become manipulated under the hand of arbitrary authority. There is, evidently, nothing more positive in the simple injunction of Jesus than there is in that of the same or the similar one of Confucius. Jesus says: "Whatsoever ye would that men should do to you, do you even so to

them." Confucius says: "Do unto another what
you would he should do unto you; and do not unto
another that you would not should be done unto
you," or as Dr. Legges has it: "What you do not
like done when done to yourself, do not do to
others." The additional sentence, that "this is the
law and the prophets," as given in the Scriptures,"
or, "thou needest but this law alone" as given in
the moral saying of "Confucius," really has nothing to do with the precept. It is simply a volun-
teered statement as to the value of the doctrine,
and is as much as to say, that as a rule of faith or
as a law, it was sufficient and could not be super-
seded.

As a fundamental principle, any person will
concede that to do wisely or to do well is to do
righteously; or, in other words, to do what is
right is to avoid doing wrong. Neither Christ
or Confucius have said more. In fact, the axiom
of the Golden Rule, as attributed to either one, is
subject to be seriously criticised. As a rule of
unquestionable action it can not be obeyed as
given in the words of either. No doubt the essential or basic idea is correct as well in the one
case as in the other.

The impressions of people are so at variance in
regard to the same thing, that it is impossible to
do unto others as you would like to have others
do unto you. In fact, if you were to do unto
others as you would have others do to you, you
would do to others what would offend, in many
instances, their sense of propriety—of right and
wrong.

The world has many curious notions in regard

to what constitutes well as, likewise, ill-doing. One person would feel offended at what another person would enjoy. One would feel exalted under the same influence that another would realize as low and degrading. Mtesa, an African king, was offended because one of his royal wives plucked and handed him a delicious fruit. He said "it was the first time a woman ever had the impudence to offer him anything," and he had her dragged off for execution.*

Most people would think that they were "doing as they would be done by" in the bestowment of a desirable gift, and certainly very few persons would be offended at such a mark of favor. But as was said of the old lady, when she kissed the cow, "There is no accounting for taste;" and we should add much less for the "decisions of judgment" as rendered by the weak and captious in mind.

We are not disposed to undervalue the real merit of any highly moral doctrine, but in this age of enlightened thought, when men are far more discerning than they were in the days of the Apostles, or in still earlier times, it may not be expected that the literary make-up of ideas should escape without comment, neither that the claimants to "moral honor" should be passed by simply on the dicta of a personal assurance that this or that matter is *all right.*

Probably the best rendering of the text which we are considering, taking the words "all things" into account, would be that adopted by some of our best writers, thus: "*Do unto another that*

* Speke and Grant's travels in Africa.

which ye would that another should do unto you under similar circumstances."

Here we have the leniency of the law. It is like the masonic idea of the "compass and the square" regulating human conduct. In other words it is the true doctrine of the "Mein" as taught by "Confucius," and may be obeyed ; whereas the axiom, as given in our commonly received versions of the New Testament Scriptures, can not by any possibility be literally fulfilled. Dr. Adam Clark virtually admits this to be true, in commenting upon this passage as written in St. Matthew, seventh chapter and twelfth verse. He says : "None but he whose heart is filled with love to God and all mankind, can keep this precept, either in its *spirit* or *letter*."

We have said enough concerning the literal construction of this text to convince any candid thinker that it is hardly possible to compound a sentence or paragraph so as to cover the whole ground of our moral needs, or one which will answer as a perfect standard for the regulation of human conduct.

The truth is, man's knowledge of right and wrong, his conception of what constitutes justice in dealing with the world, is not as easily mistaken as the meaning of words or the phraseology of a sentence, and as in the one case he need seldom if ever be mistaken, it is quite certain, that in the other, he is likely to be led astray through a misconstruction or misinterpretation of the definitive meaning of words.

As to whether Jesus or Confucius presented the axiom of the Golden Rule in the most positive form, is a question, it would seem, of no material importance; but the idea as to which presented it in the *best* form, as applied to the universal moral interests of mankind, there is something essential. A minister's opinion in regard to it, is nothing more than an expression of a personal conviction in reference to the matter; and as most clergymen see a "black sheep" whenever they think it necessary, we may not wonder at the decision of your clerical friend, that "the Golden Rule was never given until Christ gave it," or that "all other analogous sayings were merely negative utterances."*

---

* For the axiom of the Golden Rule, or other similar moral sayings, among Jewish, Christian and heathen nations, see *Wetstein's Notes.*

OUR APIARY,

The subscriber is likely to have for sale two or three hundred

SWARMS OF BEES,

in the early part of the coming autumn. To those who desire to engage in Apiculture, or who would like to keep a few Swarms for pleasure, or the honey which they gather, we shall offer a fine opportunity to purchase. Our stocks are unusually large and strong, being mixe.

AMERICAN AND ITALIAN BEES.

To those purchasing five or more Swarms, we will reveal our

SECRET OF VENTILATION,

which is the greatest *desideratum* in Winter management. This process is a sure guarantee against the loss of Swarms in the coldest latitudes in which Bees are found, as well as against the depletion of their numbers and strength, during the winter months. Our prices will range as follows:

For Two Swarms, with Winter Boxes,	-	-	$22.00
" " " without "	-	-	-	20.00
" Six " with "	-	-	60.00
" " " without "	-	-	-	54.00
" Ten " with "	-	-	100.00
" " " without "	-	-	-	90.00

All Swarms will be safely guarded by Wire Screens, for transportation, and delivered on the cars free of expense. For further particulars address the undersigned, enclosing postage stamp.

MARCENUS WRIGHT,
MIDDLEVILLE, MICH.

THE
MASTEREON.
OR
REASON AND RECOMPENSE.

———

The author met with a misfortune in publishing the above named work. Through a circumstance over which he had no control, it was put into the press without a revision of the "proofs." Although the book contains quite a number of typographical and other errors, it is nicely bound and very readable. It contains about 300 pages, in which is given a wonderful narrative of personal experience in Somnambulism and Clairvoyance, interspersed here and there by suggestive ideas and opinions. We have only about 150 copies of the first edition of 1,000 left. The price heretofore has been $1.25. We will sell the few remaining copies for $1.00 each. Postage free.

Address,

MARCENUS WRIGHT,

MIDDLEVILLE, MICH.